Cthulhu
Lovecraftian Tales From Wales

EDITED BY MARK HOWARD JONES
FOREWORD BY S. T. JOSHI
ILLUSTRATIONS BY KATE EVANS

Screaming Dreams

FIRST EDITION
- 2013 -

Published by
Screaming Dreams

113-116 Bute Street, Cardiff Bay,
Cardiff, CF10 5EQ, South Wales, UK

www.screamingdreams.com

ISBN : 978-1-906652-21-0

CONTENTS

FOREWORD
S. T. Joshi

"Of living creators of cosmic fear raised to its most artistic pitch, few if any can hope to equal the versatile Arthur Machen." That is the beginning of H. P. Lovecraft's celebrated discussion of Machen in "Supernatural Horror in Literature" (1927), a discussion that has probably prompted many readers to probe the work of this classic Anglo-Welsh writer.

Lovecraft, who first discovered Machen in 1920, went on to remark that the poignant novel *The Hill of Dreams* (1907) features a "youthful hero [who] responds to the magic of that ancient Welsh environment which is the author's own, and lives a dream-life in the Roman city of Isca Silurum, now shrunk to the relic-strown village of Caerleon-on-Usk." This comment points to one of the central reasons for Lovecraft's fondness for Machen – their joint fascination with the ancient Roman presence in Britain. Lovecraft, who from the age of five onward had nurtured himself on classical myths, Greek and Latin literature, and ancient history, found an ineffable thrill in envisioning the march of the Roman legions throughout the civilised world of two millennia ago, and perhaps envied Machen's physical proximity to the abundant Roman ruins in England, Scotland, and Wales.

Lovecraft went on to purchase many of Machen's books, including his three poignant autobiographies, *Far Off Things* (1922), *Things Near and Far* (1923), and *The London Adventure*

1

(1924). It was from these books, clearly, that Lovecraft gained a knowledge of Machen's youth in Wales and his departure from the land of his birth to become a struggling writer and journalist on Fleet Street. But of course, Lovecraft was chiefly interested in the bountiful array of Machen's weird fiction, ranging from the novella "The Great God Pan" (1894) to the episodic novel *The Three Impostors* (1895) to the landmark collection *The House of Souls* (1906). It is this last volume that contains "The White People," which Lovecraft came to rank as second only to Algernon Blackwood's "The Willows" as the greatest tale in all weird literature.

The influence of Machen on Lovecraft – and specifically on the Cthulhu Mythos – is immense, and far beyond the scope of this brief foreword. Suffice it to say that Machen's conception of a secret race of stunted, primitive beings (the "little people") dwelling on the underside of civilisation helped to trigger Lovecraft's own ideas of baleful entities lurking in forgotten corners of the world. Lovecraft had come upon Machen's fiction a few years before he read Margaret Murray's *Witch-Cult in Western Europe* (1921), which appeared to give a scholarly imprimatur to the idea of the "little people"; indeed, he went on to admit that the story "The Festival" (1923) was jointly influenced by Machen and Murray.

Machen undoubtedly influenced the seminal story of the Cthulhu Mythos, "The Call of Cthulhu" (1926). Here, a professor – and subsequently his great-nephew, after the professor dies under mysterious circumstances – ends up piecing together "dissociated knowledge" about the secret cult of Cthulhu, in very much the manner in which Professor Gregg, in "Novel of the Black Seal" (the chief episode in *The Three Impostors*), gathers together evidence of the continuing existence of the "little people." Gregg too dies mysteriously, and Lovecraft quotes with relish the professor's final warning: "If I unhappily do not return from my journey, there is no need to conjure up here a picture of the awfulness of my fate."

Machen's most obvious influence on Lovecraft occurs in "The Dunwich Horror" (1928), where the basic framework of the story – the impregnation of a woman by a "god" – is copied directly from "The Great God Pan." It is by no means clear that Lovecraft has surpassed his mentor in this tale.

What is still more interesting is that the figure – or perhaps the myth – of Machen himself enters tangentially into Lovecraft's fiction. The character Thomas Malone, in "The Horror at Red Hook" (1925), seems to bear a strong likeness to Machen. Let us recall Lovecraft's initial description of the Brooklyn police detective:

> To Malone the sense of latent mystery in existence was always present. In youth he had felt the hidden beauty and ecstasy of things, and had been a poet; but poverty and sorrow and exile had turned his gaze in darker directions, and he had thrilled at the imputations of evil in the world. Daily life had for him come to be a phantasmagoria of macabre shadow-studies; now glittering and leering with concealed rottenness as in Beardsley's best manner, now hinting terrors behind the commonest shapes and objects as in the subtler and less obvious work of Gustave Doré.

The mention of "ecstasy" is clearly a nod to Machen's idiosyncratic treastise *Hieroglyphics: A Note upon Ecstasy in Literature* (1902), while the mention of Beardsley points to Lovecraft's awareness that Machen, Beardsley, Oscar Wilde, and others were the dominant figures in the "Yellow Nineties," that *fin de siècle* period in England that had, to his delight, overturned the stodginess of Victorian conventionality and introduced a modicum of radicalism, daring, and even decadence into British culture and society.

Another possible portrayal of Machen appears in the fragment "The Descendant" (1927?), where a "man who screams when the church bells ring" is said to live in Gray's Inn, where Machen himself lived for a time. Lovecraft goes on to say of this individual, Lord Northam, that "During the 'nineties he dabbled in Satanism, and at all times he devoured avidly any doctrine or theory which seemed to promise escape from the close vistas of science and the dully unvarying laws of Nature." This is unquestionably a reference to Machen's own hostility to the relentless march of scientific knowledge and his fear – a plausible one, as it happens – that the pillars of religion might be shaken by the advance of science. Lord Northam's mind has been shattered by a reading of the *Necronomicon,* and it would have been fascinating if Lovecraft had completed this tale and explained *why* Northam had ended up as one who "lives all alone with his streaked cat... and people call him harmlessly mad."

It is a shame that Lovecraft did not pursue his readings in other Welsh writers. He would no doubt have been surprised and intrigued to learn that his great contemporary Dylan Thomas had dabbled in weird fiction from time to time, and he would surely have found much interest in the mainstream work of Caradoc Evans (1878–1945), who – like Richard Llewellyn in *How Green Was My Valley* (1939) – evoked the richness of the Welsh landscape as vividly as Lovecraft had enlivened his New England environment in such tales as "The Whisperer in Darkness" or "The Shadow over Innsmouth."

And Lovecraft would no doubt have been delighted that the Welsh authors of today have used his Cthulhu Mythos as a springboard for imaginative extrapolations of their own, as he himself had done with the weird fiction of Arthur Machen. He would have been gratified that writers of such an ancient land, where the tread of Roman legions can still be sensed, had found inspiration in his tales of cosmic horror – a meeting of minds across the water that would have heartened this scion of Devon ancestry who drew continual imaginative nourishment from the literature of Great Britain.

— S. T. JOSHI

INTRODUCTION
Mark Howard Jones & Steve Upham

The fact that the word 'Lovecraftian' can now be used to denote an entire sub-genre of literature is significant in that it indicates a rare degree of acceptance and influence. When a writer becomes a mini industry, you know he's arrived.

This is particularly remarkable if you consider that Lovecraft, at the time of his death in 1937 at the age of just 46, was virtually unknown outside of a relatively small group of friends and readers. Indeed, he hadn't had a single book published during his lifetime.

It was the devotion of his friends (in particular August Derleth) that kept alive his reputation and carefully nurtured it.

And whether you interpret Lovecraft's creations literally as many-tentacled terrors rising threateningly from the depths, or as metaphors for the existential dread that seems to dog mankind's every forward step, it is clear that he created a potent series of symbols. They have a strong grip on the imagination, spawning innumerable reprints of his own tales, numerous imitators, learned treatises on his work and even an appearance (albeit thinly disguised) in a popular cartoon about a talking dog and his mystery-obsessed young friends.

In short, he and his creations can now be found everywhere. As the French author Michel Houellebecq noted in 1998 in his book 'Lovecraft: Against the World, Against Life', "... his originality appears to me to be greater today

5

than ever." It is an originality that has some of its roots in Welsh soil.

Caerleon-born author Arthur Machen influenced Lovecraft strongly with his tales of ancient evil. Anyone who has stayed in Wales for any length of time can feel that it is an old country; very old. Machen's genius was to suggest that maybe some previous tenants of this land might not be ready to relinquish their claim on it completely. His tales impart a dreadful sense of being watched. And by something that we don't fully understand.

What Lovecraft took from Machen were these 'demoniacal hints of the truth' (as Lovecraft put it in his 1920 story 'Arthur Jermyn'), of the ancient reaching forward threateningly into the present. He then imbued them with a cosmic scale.

It could even be suggested that Lovecraft's inter-dimensional beings are versions of the Welsh myth of the *Tylwyth Teg* (or 'Fair Family'), reflected in a monstrous magnifying mirror. Machen used these supernatural beings, who were said to dwell underground or below water, in his own work (most notably in 'The White People', 'The Novel Of The Black Seal' and 'The Children Of The Pool'), making them even more terrifying than their already unsettling reputation. Perhaps Lovecraft was impressed by these creatures' reputed ability to use water as an occult gateway between their own realm and ours, echoing this in his own creations' thankfully unsuccessful attempts to create their own gateways between the arcane and the mundane.

Machen's reputation has undergone a renaissance in the last 30 years (partly – but not wholly – down to a 'reflected glory' from Lovecraft's popularity). He is now rightly regarded as one of the most important progenitors of the modern 'weird tale'. Without him, Lovecraft's work would have been very different. If he hadn't discovered Machen's tales, the Anglophile New Englander would probably have been far more influenced by Lord Dunsany or Algernon Blackwood and perhaps his writing would have had far less impact than it has had.

Given that such a large part of Lovecraft's literary DNA

came from this part of the world, it is surprising that so few Welsh authors have responded directly to his work, rather than merely being influenced by it at first or second hand. Hopefully this anthology will go some way to redressing that.

Each of the writers whose work you will find here have risen to the challenge by giving the ideas and aesthetics behind Lovecraft's Cthulhu Mythos their own distinctive twist. Whether you're looking for adventurous absurdism, punishing post-Modern puns, hallucinogenic horror or good old fashioned gooseflesh – or anything in between – you'll find it all in these pages.

Our contributors have all been born in Wales or have lived here for some time, so we hope a uniquely Welsh point of view comes through in the writing. We would like to thank all the writers for their hard work and hope this volume will provide an interesting and worthwhile addition to the canon of Lovecraftian literature.

As for that tongue-twisting title – for those unfamiliar with the Welsh language, Cymraeg is the Welsh word for 'Welsh'. A rough guide to pronunciation is Come – Rye – then a hard G (as in 'gag'), with the emphasis on the second syllable. (As far as pronouncing 'Cthulhu' is concerned, we suggest you consult the Notes On Pronunciation in the appendix of Abdul Alhazred's The Necronomicon.)

Finally, we would like to thank S. T. Joshi, the renowned Lovecraft scholar and the great man's biographer, for agreeing to write the illuminating and fascinating preface to this volume.

— Mark Howard Jones & Steve Upham, Cardiff,
September 2013

WHAT OTHERS HEAR
John Llewellyn Probert

The world is thinner in some places.

Occasionally we may encounter signs that warn us of these locations, where reality is brittle and all that we understand has the consistency of little more than tissue paper. Often, however, there is nothing obvious, and we have to rely on the instinct we have developed through millions of years of evolution, the instinct that tells us to beware, to stay away, to leave well alone, even though the so-called higher parts of our brains can conceive of no logical reason why we might feel this way. Sometimes we are so distracted by the woes and hardships of everyday life that our instincts become dulled, our minds so occupied with the mundane that we fail to realise the dangers we are exposing ourselves to. But we ignore such warnings at our peril.

Where a land steeped in myth meets an ocean witness to more tragedy than the human mind can bear, our world is especially thin. The barriers have been worn away by the incessant play of illogical horrors, of fates unexplained, of desperate longing at the unfairness of life. It should come as no surprise that in such places the waves have a song to sing, a song that is heard by the surrounding hills as they wait for that which slumbers beneath them to awaken, a song that will not be finished until time itself ends. If the light is at just the right angle, and one looks carefully, one might see patterns in the troubled waters, and in the sand, too – unnatural configurations that change every day, symbols and messages left for races long gone, and with only the merest trace memory of how to interpret them inherited by those who believe they are now the dominant species on this planet.

In these special places those whom society might kindly describe as being of a sensitive disposition need to take special care, lest the assault on their already finely-tuned senses should be too much for them, driving them into an abyss of madness from which there is little chance of return.

In some places, the sensitive must take special care.

And there are some places they should never go.

William Martin came to the seaside town of Llanroath to convalesce.

He chose it for a number of reasons. One was that he had spent many summers on the coast of South Wales as a boy, the trips to the Gower peninsula and to Carmarthenshire with his parents still amongst his fondest memories, and he hoped he might find some comfort from a part of the world that was, for the most part, familiar to him. Second, Llanroath was small, tiny in fact, and as he attributed his recent breakdown in part to the pressures of big city life he felt a break from it would also do him some good. Third, and perhaps the most decisive, Llanroath had a church in need of an organist. While he was aware that it had been in part his employment in a similar role at Bristol Cathedral that had driven him to his current state of malady, he could not be without music and besides, it was more the administrative and political aspects of the post, not to mention some of the dreadful children he had been required to teach and their even more dreadful parents, that he cited as the true cause of his breakdown. The works of Bach, Mendelssohn and Vierne hardly deserved to have the accusatory finger pointed at them as being the cause of his temporary insanity.

"You should probably take a break from the music completely for a while anyway," his psychiatrist Dr Montague had instructed.

His ENT consultant had told him the very opposite.

"There's no real way of curing tinnitus," Mr Ramply-

Watson had explained, his blue eyes bright beneath the circular examination mirror strapped to his forehead. Martin had always wondered which doctors actually wore that alien-looking thing and now he knew. "What you have to do is find ways of either blocking it out or blending it in with everyday sounds. It may sound strange, but even though your exposure to loud music was most likely the cause of the problem in the first place it's probably going to be the best palliative for your condition as well."

Of course it had been difficult to believe. Not so much the part about palliation: Martin had always considered his music to be a panacea, a welcome salve for the wounds of everyday life. It was more the fact that it had been the cause of the constant and persistent ringing in his ears from which he now suffered in the first place. Surely such a condition was the province of machine operators and heavy metal music fanatics?

"You have a demonstrable degree of deafness," the specialist had said, pointing to lines on the audiogram printout that meant nothing to Martin. "And from your history I can determine no risk factors other than the fact that for much of your life you have listened to far more music than the average human being, some of it no doubt louder than is strictly safe. I agree that it's rare for someone to suffer deafness from the kind of music you say you listen to, but it's always possible that your auditory nerves are more sensitive than others, and that they are more prone to damage than one might normally expect." Mr Ramply-Watson had put down his pen and given Martin a hard stare, "Either way, the fact of the matter is that you have partial hearing loss and that is the most likely cause of your tinnitus. I don't think a hearing aid is going to do much good, but there are other treatments available and we can explore those. In the meantime background music will probably help. As long as it's not too loud."

As is sometimes the nature of the medical profession, especially of those in different specialties, Dr Montague the psychiatrist had objected to this, but not as vehemently as Mr Ramply-Watson had proposed it. After all, aggression tends not to be part of the nature of a doctor of mental health, but he did voice his concerns in slightly louder tones than usual.

"It could be the music that was the cause of your breakdown in the first place," he said as Martin shifted uncomfortably in his chair. "Not necessarily the listening to it, but the constant requirements of your job, the need to perform perfectly those intricate five-part organ sonatas you told me about, the constant complaints from parents who felt you weren't doing your job properly, the pupils themselves who either refused or were unable to rise to your very exacting standards. Your auditory hallucinations, your feelings of frustration and low self-esteem, all of these have most likely arisen from your everyday working practice. Take a break." The psychiatrist had crossed his legs at this point. Perhaps, Martin had thought, it was his way of emphasising a point. "Take a break and get away from it all, somewhere you can feel safe. The medication I've prescribed will help with the worst of your symptoms, but it's the change of environment that will do you the world of good."

The change of environment.

William Martin arrived in Llanroath early on a Wednesday evening, the bus that took him south from Carmarthen railway station having been delayed by an accident just two miles from his destination. It was a hot day, even for late May, and it was with breathless relief that he was finally able to escape the baked air and step down onto the deserted main street. It wasn't yet dark, and the clouds in the twilit sky above him were like black ink in blue water. The bus pulled away, leaving him alone, the gentle breeze blowing sufficient to block out the tinnitus that was threatening to return, now he no longer had the sound of the vehicle's engine to keep it at bay.

Martin put down his case and rubbed his temples. To his left the street disappeared into darkness. Further on was a hill the silhouette of which he could just make out, as well as the crooked crenellations of the ruined castle that he guessed must be perched at its summit. To his right the street led to a T-junction running perpendicular, and on the other side of this T stood the pub where he had booked a room.

The Rugged Cross was tiny and ancient, and so was the cramped attic room in which Martin found himself after being guided up two flights of creaking stairs of reasonable width, and then up a third staircase that had to be the narrowest ever contrived by an architect. The landlord's name was Meillir Harris. He seemed pleasant enough as he apologised, explaining that the tavern's other rooms were occupied at present, but that as soon as a larger one became available, Martin would be moved. Martin thanked the man, who seemed as relieved to leave the room as Martin was to finally have space to move within it. The sloping roof meant that he could only stand up straight if he stood in the very middle, and the single bed with its unwelcoming-looking grey blanket creaked when he sat down. A tiny window set just below the apex of the roof gave him a view, but he would have to wait until tomorrow to see what it was. Right now, the splintered wooden frame enclosed merely darkness made all the blacker by the light of the bare bulb that hung from the ceiling. Opposite the bed, which filled one side of the room, a rickety wooden bureau provided space for Martin to unpack. The three drawers were lined with newspaper yellow with age and tinged with dots of mould, and so it surprised him to read the date on one of the spread out pages as being just last month.

The tiny bathroom was two floors down and Martin witnessed not a soul as he made his way there and back again. He had not eaten since lunchtime but found his appetite lacking after the events of the rest of the day, and so he decided to make an early night of it.

There was nowhere to plug in his white noise generator.

The thorough search Martin performed of the entire room failed to yield a single plug socket, and so the device he had been provided by the hospital's ENT department went back into its box as Martin's anxiety rose a few notches.

How was he going to stop the ringing sounds now?

They were always worse at night. Everything was always worse at night. It was in the unyielding darkness that he had finally had his breakdown as the whispering, piercing noises that had plagued him for weeks had finally resolved themselves into whispered words he could not ignore. While Dr Montague had assured him the medication he was on would keep the voices at bay, the thought of a night alone with nothing but silence terrified him.

Once Martin knew he was too scared to undress and get into bed, and that if he were to stay in that room his symptoms of mounting panic would only worsen, he realised there was only one alternative.

Despite the lateness of the hour, he would explore the town.

The landlord was calling last orders as Martin passed through the tiny bar. The two customers refused to be distracted from their cloudy beer, and even the landlord seemed unconcerned by behaviour that must surely have looked strange to them.

The main street was deserted, and the light breeze made just enough sound to distract Martin from the noises that were beginning to build inside his head. It wouldn't last, though, and Martin knew that soon the tinny whispering would become loud enough to upset him.

Where could he go?

The moon was out now, and the silhouette he had first mistaken for a castle was now bathed in silver, revealing the crenellations to belong to a bell tower, the crooked walls to be merely the angle at which the little church was positioned on the hill, much closer to the village than Martin had imagined.

There was a light on inside.

His mind made up, and with the night still warm, Martin set off up the main street, the lamps seeming to flicker in time with the whispering inside his head as he passed. Soon the buildings and the lights were gone and the road had narrowed to a single track lane. A cloud passed over the upper half of the moon, like a mask attempting to cloak a damaged mind, and Martin found himself groping in semi-darkness, his only guide the dull glow from the church.

By trial and error and several collisions with damp undergrowth, Martin discovered that the road curved round to the right and, as it crested a hill, it ended at the low stone wall of the cemetery. As if to reward his efforts, the moon suddenly divested itself of its coverings and he was allowed a metallic-grey view of the cold, unyielding building before him.

The gate in the stone wall swung open at his touch. In the darkness of the lane Martin had walked as fast as he could. Now he could see where he was going, his footsteps were more cautious, perhaps because whatever might be watching would now also be able to see him. He made his way along the gravel path that led to the door. The church was bigger than he had expected. It looked fourteenth century and had probably been built at a time when its congregation would have numbered over a hundred from the local farming and seafaring communities. Martin approached the door with a mixture of trepidation and indecision. What was he going to say to whomever he found inside? Would there be anyone in there? Was leaving a light on in the local church a custom in these parts? A traditional guiding of the lost soul to the sanctity and protection of the Lord?

Or could there be some other reason?

Martin had scarcely had time to consider this when he realised that now there was no light within the church. The dull glow that had guided him after the moon's temporary abandonment had now vanished.

The vibrations within his head were starting to make themselves known again now that he had stopped walking, the silence of the evening the perfect canvas for their delicate, insidious brushstrokes of paranoia. Martin ignored what he thought he could hear and rattled the door handle, emboldened now by the presumed absence of anyone within.

It took a little struggling, and for a moment he thought the door was locked, but eventually it creaked open to reveal a panoply of pews awash with ethereal silver-tinged shades of ruby, emerald and sapphire from the moonlight's passage through the stained glass of the windows opposite.

Martin took a step inside and the door banged shut behind him. It made him jump but, once he appreciated that it had failed to arouse the interest of anyone who might be in the building with him, it was in a slightly more relaxed state that he proceeded up the aisle to where he could see the organ, positioned to the left of the altar.

It looked open.

He could see the manuals, two of them, arranged in

stepwise fashion, the protective wooden shutter that one would normally expect to be locked over them slid back to also reveal the organ stops that were arranged in two corresponding rows above the two sets of keyboards.

The sounds in his head were more piercing now, like wire being scratched across steel, the grating tones resolving themselves into words that told him how useless he was, how worthless, how he could never succeed in anything. He would never have thought the word 'failure' could sound so abrasive until he began to hear it inside his own head.

There was only one cure.

Martin located the brown power switch in its circular plastic moulding and flipped it upward.

A sound like a dragon taking a breath filled the room as the organ's working mechanism filled with air, readying itself to breathe pure music through the pipes that stood proud above him. All it would take would be the merest touch of his fingertips, both to make the instrument before him sing, and to make the voices stop.

He sat himself on the polished wooden stool and was about to begin playing when something made him hesitate.

Made him look to his right.

Made him see the picture above the altar.

It should have been comforting, that painting. At least, Martin assumed that must have been the intention, depicting as it did Jesus Christ at the time of his crucifixion, the arms outspread, the face bloodied by the crown of thorns, the single nail through both feet pinning them to what was probably cypress wood, or so some scholars apparently believed.

It wasn't comforting, though. It wasn't comforting at all.

It was positively hideous.

As Martin stared at it he realised it wasn't so much the image of the Christ figure itself that was disturbing, but what surrounded it. Now he could see that what had initially looked like a murky fog done in unsavoury shades of charcoal grey and muddy brown actually served to conceal horrors that seemed to lurk deeper within. Martin tried hard, but he could not quite make out the shapes that he felt were crawling just beneath the paint.

But he was sure they were there.

He shook his head and looked again. It was easier to see them now, those things with tiny segmented bodies and multi-jointed limbs that seemed absurdly, supernaturally long as they plucked at the skin of the dying man on the cross.

As he watched, one of them turned and looked at him.

And spoke.

It was too much of a coincidence for it to be anything else. The high-pitched whine that pierced Martin's left ear had him clutching his skull in pain. The noise that now filled his head began to vary, as if the pointed tip of one of those insectoid claws was being dragged across his eardrum. It was all Martin could do to reach the organ stops with his right hand and blindly draw as many of them as he could before playing the first thing that came to mind.

The Bach fugue was not meant to be performed with such an inappropriate combination of pipes as he had selected, but it served to blot the worst of the ringing in his ears. Within a few bars Martin was able to open his eyes, and within a few more the scratching on the inner wall of his skull had subsided. Another line of music, and a modulation from G Minor to D Minor, and Martin realised the only thing he could now hear was the music. He relaxed but didn't stop playing. How silly he had been, how foolish, letting his tinnitus get the better of him to the extent that he had started hallucinating like that.

Without taking his fingers from the keys, Martin looked to his right to reassure himself that the picture above the altar was nothing more than the sort of image one might find in any ordinary country church.

What he saw made him scream.

The painting was bleeding.

Tiny pinpricks of dark red were erupting from the murk surrounding the crucified figure. As they coalesced they began to run down the painting, trickling over the pale form of Christ and adding crimson rivulets to the tortured body on the cross.

Martin took his fingers from the keys and swung himself off the organ stool to get a better view. Almost immediately the whining, scraping, screaming sounds were back, and this time they were much, much worse, as if the organ music had inflicted some terrible torture on the things he thought he had seen, as if it was their bodies that had broken and burst and bled as a result of his playing.

Martin tried to get back on the stool but now the noise was so bad all he could do was clutch his head and sway from side to side as the creatures screamed, as the creatures cursed him.

As the creatures swore revenge.

The nearest hospital was Glangwili General in Carmarthen, and so Martin was taken there after being discovered early the next morning collapsed in front of the altar. The doctor who saw him in the A&E department diagnosed a combination of lack of sleep, stress, and most importantly a lack of attention to his treatments and medications as having caused the episode, and Martin was discharged with the promise that he would keep any nocturnal wanderings to a minimum.

It was another baking hot day and the taxi that drove him back to Llanroath had all its windows open. Martin welcomed the breeze as the depot injection he had been given at the hospital began to do its work.

"Don't forget you've been given it," the doctor had warned. "Taking your regular medication on top of this could prove disastrous. It should last for five days and then you should start on the tablets again. And find somewhere to plug in that white noise machine!"

Back at The Rugged Cross Martin was met by the landlord and his wife, Llinos, both of whom looked worried.

"I'll be fine," Martin reassured them. "But if it's at all possible I'd like a different room."

"Of course," said Mrs Harris, taking his arm and leading him into the snug. "Meillir will sort that out for you, won't you, Meillir?"

Her husband nodded as she sat Martin down and asked him what he would like for breakfast. Martin shook his head, explaining that he was still feeling queasy from the medication he'd been given.

"Well you have to have something," the woman replied,

looking shocked. "How about some lovely eggs? And tea with lots of sugar – that should have you back on your feet in no time."

Before Martin could object she had disappeared into the back. He rubbed his eyes, stretched his arms, and looked around him at the empty seats and polished wooden tables.

He frowned. Surely if the pub was as full as Mr Harris had claimed there should have been one or two late eaters? Or at least the evidence of their passing in the form of greasy plates, toast crumbs and coffee rings on the tables?

Martin took a breath and the tang of stale beer assailed his nostrils. In the background, the pleasant clatter of Harris and his wife going about their morning duties helped to keep what little noise there was now inside his head at bay. Llinos had sat him in sunshine, and now it was beginning to hurt his eyes. He was about to move when she returned, bearing a plateful of food he knew he could never hope to consume.

"Just have as much of it as you can," she said in reaction to his shocked expression. "It'll do you good."

Martin regarded the mixture of greying scrambled eggs and crumbling rust-coloured black pudding.

"I'll try," he promised, wondering how he could turn attention away from the unappetising pile before him. Then he remembered the slip of paper in his wallet on which he had scribbled the details of who he was supposed to report to when he arrived. "Can you tell me where this is?" he said, taking it out and showing it to her.

Llinos Harris frowned as she peered at Martin's cramped handwriting. "Take a right out of here and keep going," she said. "You can't miss it. I don't know how happy he'll be to see you, though."

Martin frowned. "Why not?"

Llinos nodded at the paper again. "That's the vicar's place," she said. "And it was the vicar that found you."

Llanroath vicarage was probably the grandest building in the village. Set back in its own grounds, the Victorian redbrick could have passed for the old village school. Or, Martin thought as he approached it, the old village hospital, the kind of place where you were locked away until someone came to claim you.

If anyone ever did.

Stop thinking like that, Martin told himself as he rang the bell and waited in the drizzling rain.

Fortunately he was not left waiting, or worrying, for long.

"Are you feeling better, now?" the Reverend Idris Clements asked as he showed Martin into his study. With his stocky build and balding, bullet-shaped head that betrayed the scars of what Martin hoped were sporting injuries and nothing more serious, the vicar looked more suited to the role of a rugby international prop forward than the pastor of a small Welsh village. He motioned Martin to sit and then dropped himself into a swivel chair that creaked alarmingly as his bulk made contact with it.

"I am, thank you," Martin replied. "Although I have to say I am rather embarrassed, especially as I've come here to be your new organist."

"Have you now?" The vicar grinned and there was a glint in his eye. "So what exactly were you doing? Getting a bit of practice in before you came to see me?"

Martin could feel his heart pounding against his chest. "Actually," he said, "there are probably a few things I should explain about myself."

The vicar was very understanding which, when Martin thought about it later, was hardly surprising. Of course, he only mentioned his medical diagnoses and omitted the bit about the hallucinations he'd had last night.

Clements steepled his fingers. "And music stops these...voices, does it?" he said.

Martin nodded. "Lots of types of sound will, but I'm sure you can understand why the organ works the best."

The vicar nodded while reaching into his right hand desk drawer. He took out a small bunch of keys and tossed them over. "These should get you into the church and the organ whenever you feel the need to play," he said. "I can't explain why you were able to get into the church so late the other night, nor why the organ had been left open." He gave Martin a beatific smile. "Perhaps the Lord had something to do with it," he said.

Clements rose to indicate their meeting was over, and Martin followed him into the hallway.

And gasped as he saw the picture hanging there.

There was nothing in what was depicted that shocked him. It was a landscape painting, probably of somewhere local, depicting rolling hills curling around a sandy beach. No, it was not what was depicted.

It was the style of the picture.

The whole thing had been rendered in the same murky colours as the background of the painting of Christ in the church. The mountains had not been coloured the vibrant emerald of a summer's day, but rather the muddy, unappetising green of midwinter. The sand was the colour of old flesh, washed out and dying. But the strangest thing was that it was obviously meant to depict a view through a window while a storm was raging. The sky was so clogged with thick grey clouds that the heavy raindrops looked filthy against the glass, and Martin could almost feel the wind rattling the pane of the picture's frame.

"That's quite an...odd picture," Martin said, trying to find a word that wasn't too damning.

"Local artist," said Clements. "Or rather he was. You probably saw the painting he did for us behind the altar up at the church."

Martin nodded. Was it his imagination or was something moving in the murk of those black waves? Something just below the surface but yearning to break through, yearning to drag itself onto that flaccid corpse of a beach and feast on the necrotic tissue of the land.

Nonsense.

"It's a bit...grim," he said.

"I suspect he was influenced by the weather," Clements chuckled. "It does rain rather a lot here." He took a step back and cocked his head sideways. "It's called 'The Land in Anger'." He gestured at the picture. "All this roiling, swirly stuff is apparently intended to signify that whatever lives beneath the soil could one day break through if sufficiently angered."

Martin raised his eyebrows. "What's it doing in your house?" he said.

Clements shrugged. "An artist, down on his luck – what else could I do when he came calling? I bought it from him as an act of charity and gave him a commission to repaint the figure you can see behind the altar. I thought it might help his state of mind but, alas, it was not to be."

Martin didn't like the sound of that. "I'm guessing he's no longer with us?" he said.

Clements shook his head. "Despite our best efforts," he replied as he showed Martin out. "And I wouldn't want the same thing to happen to you so please, if you feel I can be of any help at all, do not hesitate to get in touch."

Martin nodded. "I promise I will," he said.

"Remember you can use the organ at any time. And if your head gives you trouble, I've been told it often helps if you write things down," the vicar gave Martin a knowing look. "I believe it is said to have a purging effect."

Martin's new room was slightly bigger, and the window that looked out over the street gave him a view of the church tower that should have reassured him but which instead he found disconcerting. His fear of what he imagined he had seen there was stronger than any comfort the building could offer.

The ringing in his ears had dulled for now. But for the occasional piercing whine he could live with it, and his white noise generator, plugged in and by the bedside, was off for the moment. He had not brought any means of playing music as he had been warned this in itself could be damaging.

So Martin sat in the near-silence, the only sounds the gentle scraping in his head mixed with the occasional vehicle passing by. On the table in front of him sat the blank exercise book he had purchased from the village newsagent's on his way back from the vicarage. His pen was yet to violate the sheer white of the paper and his thoughts were already turning to another walk, perhaps even another visit to the church – anything rather than this gaunt, maddening isolation that was meant to be recuperative but instead stood a chance of driving him more insane than the city life that had caused him to come here.

It began to rain, the heavy, filthy drops that struck the glass reminding him of the painting at the vicarage. Before he knew it, the sounds in his head were beginning to worsen as well – scraping, clawing, whining, constantly changing as if they were trying to make themselves understood.

And then he did understand.

Not everything, but enough for Martin to realise they weren't like the voices he had heard during his breakdown, or even during what had happened in the church last night. They had a different timbre, a different urgency, and most important of all, they didn't seem to be trying to destroy his self-confidence. In fact the few words he could make out were strange.

Very strange indeed.

Martin picked up his pen and began to write, if only to see if it might help. He was putting nonsense on the page – he knew that , but it didn't stop him, and as he wrote the words down the voices in his head gave him new ones. Before he realised it he had filled a page with odd combinations of letters. A few of which were familiar, most of which were unrecognisable.

And then the voices went away.

Just as it stopped raining.

Martin put down his pen, took a deep breath, and realised he felt much better. Perhaps the vicar had been right after all. He grabbed his jacket and left for the church, intending to confront the altar painting while he was still in his current state of wellbeing.

The way looked very different in the grey light of day, and as he approached the building Martin felt some of his anxiety beginning to creep back. His head was still refreshingly empty of noise, however, and this spurred him on, through the lychgate, along the path and into the building.

The picture was still there, but it looked much less threatening now. It was still as disturbing as an image of a man crucified against a murky background could be, but today Martin could not see any evidence of shapes lurking close to the body, and of course there was no blood.

Blood which had flowed in response to his playing.

Martin licked his lips and looked at the organ console, which had now been replaced and locked after the events of last night.

Of course he had the keys now, he thought, fingering them in his jacket pocket. It would only take a minute to play something, to run through a few bars of a Bach cantata and keep his eye on the picture to prove to himself that what he had seen was just the product of his tired, overworked and unhappy mind.

He unlocked the console cover, slid it back, and flicked on the power switch.

After he had drawn stops that would allow for a soft, reassuring timbre, Martin paused, his fingertips hovering over the keyboard. He took one more look at the picture, decided what he was going to play, and began.

For the first couple of minutes he didn't dare look away from the instrument, allowing the music to calm him, the repetitive lines of the fugue overlying each other, mingling and taking on new variations that were so familiar to him he could have played the piece in his sleep.

It was nearly over before Martin realised he was too scared to look up.

He finished the piece, and selected stops that would produce a more bombastic sound, as if his playing might act as a shield for what awaited him behind the altar.

He managed two pages of Bach's Fantasia in G Minor before he forced himself to turn his head to the right.

At first it was difficult to see what had happened. It was as if the entire wall behind the altar had been replaced by a black void, an empty nothingness from which not even light could escape. As Martin continued to play he realised the space below the stained glass window wasn't black at all.

It was red.

Deep red.

And now there were things coming out of it.

Martin watched in horror, his fingers still playing of their own accord, as the surface of the slick crimson was broken by multi-jointed thread-like appendages as red as the scarlet pool from which they were arising. Searching for purchase, some quickly found the grey stone on either side, while others met with the polished tiled floor, scrabbling as they attempted to lever out whatever bloated, unholy bodies were still concealed within the ghastly place from which they were attempting to escape.

Were they real? Hallucination? An effect of the drugs he had been given in the hospital? Or would they actually look even more terrifying if he hadn't been given the medication?

As more of the spider-like limbs appeared, and thread-like antennae began to probe the new, strange atmosphere, Martin realised that deliberation was not going to save him.

He slid himself off the organ stool and ran, down the aisle and out through the doors, closing them behind him in case they offered some barrier to what was coming after him.

When he turned round, the world had changed.

The sky had darkened and, worse, reddened to the point where it was almost as if he were looking up from the surface of an alien planet. Clouds that resembled amoebae crawled across the heavens, enveloping stars and leaving trails of black dust behind them.

The cemetery was still there, as was the road, and Martin tore himself toward it, turning right and heading for the sea, where he could see a few scant traces of normal blue sky on the horizon.

The road ended and became a dirt track which soon also faded away. Martin turned to see that the path he had just fled along had now vanished, and that the landscape looked different, barren, unearthly.

He clutched his temples. This could not be happening! It had to be inside his head! He turned toward the sea, towards the cliffs he knew towered there.

A lone figure was standing at the cliff's edge. As Martin got closer he realised he recognised who it was.

Idris Clements.

"You don't look too well, my boy." The vicar extended a hand as Martin approached. "You don't look too well at all."

Martin, his hands clutched to his temples, fell to his knees as he reached the man in black. He looked up to see red flooding across the sky, obliterating the last vestiges of blue. The unhealthy burnt-looking sun that now hung in the alien heaven bathed everything with pallid light, lending the landscape a sickly ochre hue that made Martin feel nauseous.

"What's happening?" he asked.

Clements shook his head. "Nothing," he replied. "Nothing to me, anyway. What might be happening to you, of course, could be an entirely different story."

Martin narrowed his eyes as the pounding in his head worsened and the light surrounding him seemed so ugly as to be almost malefic. "What do you mean?" he croaked.

"So many of them come," said Clements. "And so many of them die. All of them, eventually." He indicated the waves tearing at the rocks below. "And all of them down there."

Martin looked at the water, at the way it swirled beneath the unnatural light of the new sun, creating patterns that he could almost believe were intentional.

"They are," said Clements, as if reading his thoughts. "Or at least I believe them to be. Just another method of communication we no longer understand, like the things you, and others, have heard and seen."

Martin shook his head. "But what I could hear was just part of an illness," he said. "An imbalance of brain chemicals and electrical impulses."

"And what do you think caused those imbalances in the first place?" Clements gestured around him. "There are myths about the creatures that live beneath these hills, that slumber out there in salt water that is far deeper than anyone could ever know. But there are other myths as well, stories of the servants of these old ones who are the very opposite in terms of size. They are as tiny as their masters are vast, and are perfectly capable of crawling along nerve fibres and sending their own messages to them."

In the changing world around him the vicar was the only constant, and now Martin hung onto that desperately. "How do you know so much about them?" He looked at Clements in disbelief. "And you being a man of God!"

Clements smiled. "I'm a man who likes to be on the

winning side," he replied. "Two thousand years ago it was Christianity. Two million years ago it was beings much older even than that, and very soon they will rise again. I haven't decided which side to take yet," he added. "I'm just trying, in the fashion of the true scholar of theological matters, to gather as much information about them as possible. Which is where people like you come in."

"What do you mean, people like me?" Martin said, having to shout to be heard above the roaring of the blood-tinged surf.

"Sensitive people come here," Clements said. "They are both drawn to this place and are receptive to the things here that the less gifted amongst us are unaware of. They see and they hear, but they don't understand. That poor artist fellow was one. I tried to help channel what was revealed to him in the hope he might be able to make some sense of it, but it all became too much for him. His legacy remains, however, for the scholars amongst us to try and interpret, just as your crude attempts at describing your experiences in that notebook will be added to the increasing body of documentation we have about those that slumber beneath these hills."

"I can hear them again!" Martin was shaking now. "I can hear them, but not out here, not out in this world." He clutched at his temples. "The world has changed but I can still hear them inside my head," he moaned. "They make scratching sounds, clicks and squawks. How can I make them stop? How can I get them to realise that I don't understand them? That I'm not a part of this world they're showing me? And that I never will be?"

"Perhaps not ever," said Clements. "Perhaps all it might take is a leap of faith."

He looked down into the swirling scarlet foam below. Martin followed his gaze.

"It's the only way, you know," said Clements. "I've seen too many like you. Once it's gone this far there is only one way to stop the madness, if madness it is, rather than truth."

He helped the organist to his feet.

"That's the problem with you sensitive types," he said. "You're the only ones who can see, the only ones who can communicate, and yet it's just all too much for your minds to deal with."

Martin peered over Clements' shoulder at the vast lobulated creature towering behind him, its multifaceted eyes focused on Martin, one huge serrated claw poised to take him in its grasp.

"Whatever it is you're looking at," Clements said, "it can't see me. I haven't revealed myself to it. But you have. And there's only one way out. Unless you wish to wait for its friends to catch up with it. They want to meet you too."

That was it. That was enough. Martin took a single, deep breath, thrust himself forward into the air, and then he was gone. The waves swallowed him and left not a trace.

And on a lonely Welsh hillside beneath a sky that now threatened rain, a solitary figure made its way back to where it, and others like it, lived, to await the coming of others sensitive to the ancient horror that lurked beneath the seemingly silent landscape. Others who would be able to see, and hear, and unwittingly break down barriers that were already so thin as to be almost absent.

Almost.

THE BICYCLE-CENTAUR
Rhys Hughes

I am a bicycle-centaur. No point in pedalling about the bush. My name is Sadulsor Raleigh but it seems I'm not a descendant of that famous and fabulous pirate and explorer, Sir Walter. Too bad. It could even be the case that I wasn't born at all but created by some mad inventor somewhere in a crepuscular garage cluttered with the tools and spare parts of a true tinkerer's den.

That does seem the most likely and plausible explanation for my existence. I have met several similar beings on my varied travels, including a man-clock and a lady-waterwheel, and they too might have been designed by the same insane boffin somewhere. I have heard a name proposed, a certain Dr Mondaugen, as a candidate for the honour, and so I'm curious about him.

My tyres are large and wide enough to propel me across the most rugged and unhappy terrain with relative ease and I am fit and healthy, a fine figure of a hybrid, and I still recall with joy the commotion I caused near Aberystwyth in the dusk as I raced down the beach with a flaming pine torch held high in one hand, honking my rubber horn and scattering lovers and other night-strollers. It was fun. I'm a creature of fun, make no mistake. Dark and nasty fun.

The country of Wales is my territory, the entire land with its mountains and valleys and forests, lakes, marshes and rain. I have explored nearly every nook and cranny of this ancient realm, threaded my way down every obscure road and lane, crossed crumbling stone bridges and coasted the banks of forgotten canals and parked in the ruins of castles buried by shifting dunes. It has been an education, the only one that an entity in my condition can ever really hope for, though I did once formally apply to become a student at Lampeter University.

I was rejected, of course. They had already filled their quota of monsters and other weirdlings and didn't need any more anomalies. I wasn't too disappointed, as I had no real desire to waste years of my life reading books and revising for exams, especially as I would have to spend a good proportion of my time indoors, which is something that has never appealed to me. The Dean came to offer his condolences in person and I think he must have been embarrassed and anxious not to be branded a racist or grotesqueophobe or similar bully.

"I am sorry, Mr Raleigh, but we don't have the facilities."

"Call me Sadulsor," I said sweetly.

"Yes, well, the failure of your application has nothing to do with any tactical or political reasoning on the part of this august institution but is simply a reflection of the fact that extensive structural rearrangements would have to be made in order to give a bicycle access to the full range of services available to undergraduates. To put it another way, you wouldn't thrive here."

"August institution? But it's only June!"

"Monsters are rarely or never happy in academic circles, that's a simple fact. I am not judging you at all. I'm helping you."

"You took a werewolf as a student last year, I know."

"That's true. I'm glad you have read our prospectus. But with lycanthropes it is different; there's a tradition. Perhaps in years to come we will be able to accept a wider range of mutants and abominations than we currently do. Sadulsor, please do not take any of this personally, dear chap."

"Are you going to pull your long nose at this point?"

He blinked. "What do you mean?"

"In stories, when two characters in a superficially polite but inherently tense conversation reach an impasse, one of them generally tugs his nose. I could tug my own but feel no desire to. So it's your call."

"I won't," he said, suddenly defiant. Then he glowered.

"Farewell," I answered simply.

"Will you come back one day?" he asked.

"Yes, yes." I honked twice and accelerated away from the college grounds. I had no intention of ever returning to Lampeter and would avoid it assiduously if my random wandering ever returned me to this region. And this resolution of mine was the main cause of the bizarre adventure that happened a few seasons later, which it is my intention to recount in the following few pages. Why don't you brew yourself a cup of tea while I oil my bearings and chain?

I stopped at a lonely crossroads for a rest and to exchange news with any other odd wayfarers who might be about, which is one of our customs. The view was bracing but bleak, moorland with mountains in the distance shrouded in thick fog like warts and bunions looming out of the foam of a hag's bubble bath. A small fire was going on the verge and tea was being brewed. Some vile wanderers were squatting nearby and waiting patiently for a cuppa. I joined them.

Damon Nomad, king of the travelling palindromes, was there, but I found it difficult to decipher what he told me. It was all clever, doubtless, but too strained and contrived for my taste. I can't recall a single thing he said to me, so I won't try to give examples. I prefer one-directional talk. I was pleasant enough to him all the same, as it never pays to be rude to a monster. They know how to bear a grudge for a lifetime or longer, depending on whose life it is.

More comprehensible and forthcoming was Cassius Befuddle, a close pal of mine from way back. We had knocked about together a lot in our youth, whenever that was, for neither of us could ever be sure. Possibly the most unique entity in the known world, Cassius was an *apricorn*, in other words, half apricot, half leprecorn; and a leprecorn, as you probably know, is already half leprechaun, half unicorn, so

31

his genetic mix was deeply profound and unusual.

Cassius informed me that eldritch lights had been seen over a narrow valley not too far from Lampeter. He hadn't gone to investigate them personally, nor did he know anyone who had, but at night the lights in question danced in a way utterly unlike any known artificial illumination but they didn't seem natural either, and this fact could be deduced from a distance. He had no agenda for confiding in me and I don't think he was expecting me to go forth to look.

"Ignis fatuus," he declared.

I turned my head, misunderstanding him, thinking he was calling the name of an acquaintance, a monster that had just arrived.

"There's no one there," I said.

"Sadulsor, my gullible and charming chum, I wasn't hailing an individual but referring to the official name of those mysterious lights sometimes seen in marshes and abandoned graveyards by lost or unlucky travellers. Ignis fatuus. I was about to explain that the lights spotted over that valley *aren't* like those but utterly different and therefore doubly or triply peculiar."

"Forgive me." The truth is that I didn't truly care about the lights. They were just part of an unresolved minor anecdote to be exchanged at a crossroads while tea leaves were flavouring water in a gigantic teapot nestled among the daisies. I would forget about the story within five minutes of leaving this little gathering. I am much more interested in my own lights, my twin headlamps, which are like surplus eyes that work in reverse, throwing beams out.

Cassius knew this. "You are always forgiven."

Something else that Cassius Befuddle told me before I departed was that he too had lately sought admission to Lampeter as an undergraduate and had also been politely but firmly repelled by the Dean, who told the *apricorn* that the university had filled and exceeded its quota of monsters not only for the coming academic year, or even for the foreseeable future, but for all time.

I found this to be extraordinary news and my suspicions

were aroused, not in an erotic way, as the word 'aroused' might suggest, for that never happens, but in a honest and clean manner. Yet stronger than my suspicions was my distaste and for a second time I silently pledged never to pass through Lampeter; for in my mind the little town had become a symbol of bigotry.

Do monsters require a formal education anyway?

They don't. Ask Medusa or anyone.

But then one evening, many months later, I happened to be on the road to Lampeter again, and as I looked up and saw a sign announcing that the town lay only a short distance ahead I remembered my vow never to revisit the place. Stale anger welled up in me and turned fresh in a curious reversal of the usual decay process but I had no desire to turn back the way I had come. I hate retracing my steps, not that I have feet to make steps, but you know what I mean.

So I took a detour down the first side road I encountered.

It wasn't really a road but a rough track that obviously hadn't been used for a generation or more, but a generation of what kind of creature I couldn't say. As the sun began to set, the path faded away to nothing and I found myself bouncing over lumpy ground littered with small stones. Then I entered a forest of stunted oaks and elms that grew denser the further I penetrated it.

I had no intention of going back. "I may have to camp here."

There was no moon and the sky was overcast and my headlamps did a rather poor job at showing me the way, partly because of the mist that swirled around the twisted roots and partly because there wasn't any way to speak of anyway. I judged it to be a peaceful and uneventful forest, a place of minimal evil, until a distant and oddly guttural roar shattered my complacency on this score. It may seem laughable that a monster can be scared, but that's how it is.

My terror encouraged me to move at greater speed despite the discomfort of the uneven terrain and the danger of a collision.

Abruptly I broke out of cover and skidded to a halt on the edge of a cliff, of a precipice that overhung a narrow valley. The length of this valley was intermittently bathed with flickers and bubbles of pale light.

I say 'pale' but in fact the hue was indescribable.

The colours of the flashes were somehow simultaneously within and outside the spectrum of visible light, like a rainbow that was experimenting with meditation and psychedelic drugs and cranial electrotherapy. I was acutely aware even then, as I am now, that words are inadequate to describe this light. Why then do I persist in making an attempt? Because you expect me to try.

It quickly occurred to me that I had accidentally stumbled on the location of Cassius Befuddle's anecdote, the valley of weird lights. The roar had propelled me towards it. Later I learned the sound had issued from the maw of a saurian, a beast which this region was still infested with; but at that instant I had only one desire, a perverse urge to learn the secret of these lights, to know their true nature and report back to Cassius, thereby earning his admiration.

The admiration of an *apricorn* is not easily acquired.

I trundled carefully along the rim of the precipice in the hope of finding some safe way down; and eventually I did discover a path that had been cut into the sheer stone wall of the cliff. My sense of balance is good and I had few problems making my way to the bottom of the gorge, the eerie flickering washing my face in photons as decadent as any emitted by the most satanic star in any galaxy in the universe. In less than half an hour I had reached the bottom.

Or maybe the bottom reached me first.

I don't mean to be obscure. I'm a bicycle-centaur and therefore not noted for an aptitude for word games. It just seemed to me that I was on the valley floor long before I should have been, as if the ground below had risen up to meet me coming down, a gesture of geological courtesy truly disturbing in its seismic implications. I rested for a minute before proceeding. And then—

The figure that greeted me was half statue, half slime mould.

"You may not pass," it said.

"That is true, but on the other hand I may," I answered.

"On the other *hand*?" A sneer.

"The other handle." I corrected myself.

"No, I will prevent you."

"You might prevent me, and then again you might not."

"I'm sure I will, very sure."

And it opened its jaws extremely wide like a snake trying to eat a rugby ball and shouted the following irrelevant words, "I had a really good wash followed by a thorough scrub, but my nose still smells."

Not only were these words irrelevant and humorous, mildly so, but they were harmless too, and yet I found myself recoiling in alarm as every separate syllable of what he uttered burst into fire while my ears were digesting them. The sound waves became visible, sheets of peculiar flame that alternately contracted and expanded in mid air and rushed up the valley and took off into the sky, the afterglow lingering a long time like some sort of evil aurora borealis.

"I don't understand," I said.

"When I was at school I was a milk monitor. A milk monitor lizard," said the figure, and these words also turned into pale flames that crackled and hissed around me and photographed the grimacing rocks.

"Your joke caught fire," I announced lamely.

"A pun went to a theatre to see a play, a wordplay. 'The performance was a joke,' it said afterwards," cried the figure.

These words also flared and glittered and dazzled.

"Who said afterwards?" I wailed.

"The pun did," replied the figure, then it snarled, "I used to be lazy but since I acquired a chauffeur I've been a driven man." More flames. "I was told to 'show my feelings' so my anger did a tap-dance."

"You are roasting the entire valley," I rebuked him.

"During a recent insurrection I was condemned to be 'shot on the spot' but I had unblemished skin that day so I survived..."

"Please stop it!" I chattered.

"I sometimes feel that my efforts in the factory that makes work surfaces for kitchens are counter-productive," came next.

I knew that whatever the melting point of my chassis was, the melting point of my mind was lower. Already my thoughts were turning sticky; soon they would turn to liquid and trickle down inside each other and blend into a chaotic mess that would be the end of my consciousness, my soul. I lowered my head in a gesture of total submission and shut my eyes tight; and the figure seemed to accept this as the signal to cease combusting the night so weirdly.

"I am the new guardian of Lladloh," he explained.

"No idea what that means," I said.

"The village of Lladloh lies at the far end of this valley and my job is to stop strangers entering. This is the only easy approach, so I have been posted here like a sentry. I deter intruders with flaming quips."

"Ah, so that is what they are. It's an unusual technique."

The figure nodded and sighed.

"To be perfectly frank, I think the inventor who created me made a mistake. I believe he intended to arm me with a flaming *whip* but the specification was written down incorrectly in his blueprints. When he came to the task of putting me together he didn't bother to adjust the error. It's not the first time he has done something like this. That's exactly the kind of lunatic he is."

"The quips are ferociously effective deterrents anyway."

He shrugged. "I suppose so."

"May I have the pleasure of knowing your name?"

"I have already told you. It is Perfectly Frank. My inventor is none other than the great Dr Karl Mondaugen, the finest non-biological father a monster could ever hope to have! He is in the middle of conducting an abstruse ritual in the village and outsiders would surely disrupt the delicate procedure. Thus I must repel all attempts to enter Lladloh, whether by men, dinosaurs or other beings. Now I will urge you to turn around and go back the way you came."

"Mondaugen, you say? Dr Mondaugen! He is my father too!"

And I honked my horn twice.

Perfectly Frank regarded me with the cold granite stare of a statue that knows how wicked are the ways of all sentient entities, how treacherous and deceitful, and he lifted a slimy arm to point at me. "Truly?"

"I think so. It's a possibility at least! Let me through, please, that I may visit him and ask the question directly and put my weak mind at rest, for I am but a poor velocipede-human hybrid, an orphan with twelve gears and no prospects who wants only to establish his origins so that when he finally dies, weary and rusty, he can at least say to himself, 'Yes, I was the son of a mighty man, the brainchild of the fine Mondaugen, an inventor rarer than the element technetium, which certainly isn't to be had in large quantities at all anywhere.'"

Perfectly Frank rubbed his flinty chin in thought.

"I don't know," he said at last.

There was an uncomfortable silence that needed to be broken. I decided, like a mallet striking a plate, to do the breaking.

"What is the abstruse ritual he is engaged upon?" I asked.

"He hopes to summon OOTOO."

"I have not heard of this personage. Is he a celebrity?"

"OOTOO is an acronym. It stands for One of the Old Ones. You know what the Old Ones are, I take it? There are very many of them. I won't try to list all their names or we will be here for many weeks."

"Yes, I know. Which of the Old Ones does he plan to call?"

"I would prefer not to say."

"Is it Cthulhu himself? Is it Azathoth, Nyarlathotep, Yog-Sothoth, Ithaqua, Aphoom-Zhar, Dagon, Zoth-Ommog, Tsathoggua, Yig, Shub-Niggurath, Plonker, Ghatanothoa or Hastur the Unspeakable?"

Perfectly Frank actually shuddered!

"Well, coincidentally, the name of the one he has chosen is Ootoo. What are his motives for doing such a perverse thing? I think he is tired of the duplicity of men and women and wants to teach them a lesson, to punish them, humiliate them. The arrival of Ootoo will achieve that aim."

I was compelled to agree that it would, absolutely.

Somehow I persuaded Perfectly Frank to let me pass and I trundled onward into the village. I think he must have recognised something about me that proved to his own satisfaction that we were brothers. He was taking a big risk doing this, certainly, for it meant dereliction of duty; and there was no judging how agonisingly the inventor might decide to punish a slime mould statue.

I'll always remember Perfectly Frank as a good sort.

As I left, he shouted out a last quip, a joke or warning. "I was sold down the river in the current financial crisis and I'm not sure *weir* I've ended up." The flames of that crackle-danced around my back wheel.

And then I was accelerating down a narrow road and crossing a stone bridge to the sound of a lonely saxophone, for there was a musician who dwelled under it, a cannibal by the name of Toby, but he plays no further part in this story. Not sure why I even mentioned him, but it *was* melancholy music, the jazz he played on that bloodstained sax, and it did influence my mood.

Suffused with sweet woe, I skidded into the main square.

I suppose I was half mad at that particular instant, rushing to discover if the rumour of my parentage was true or not. It scarcely mattered where I came from, to be blunt, for I was incapable of producing any descendants. There were no female bicycle-centaurs anywhere else in the world.

That, at any rate, was the consensus of the time.

Lately there has been speculation by trustworthy philosophers that there *is* a realm where beings like me flourish. But I'm digressing again. Let me backpedal to the point of my entry into the village square.

One side of the space, the side directly facing me, was formed by the bulk of a vast and ancient tavern, a higgledy-piggledy edifice with crazy wild boars for the piggles and demented crocodilians for the higgles. This tavern was none other than the notorious Nameless Tavern in which so many of Lladloh's dark, odd, curiously peculiar and contrived deeds were first plotted, then enacted and finally analysed, a labyrinth of beery doom and wormy trepidation.

And gathered in front of the door was a motley collection of faded characters that had all the appearance of people on the way to becoming phantoms while still alive. Rather, they were like fictional personages in books that are rarely read, that are hardly known enough even to be forgotten.

One of them was a man who creaked and whirred like a skeleton clock as he stepped forward to intercept me; but I had already come to a dead halt and posed no threat to this etiolated mob. Then another man, burly but slack of skin, shook jowls as grey as the jackets of boring business suits flapping on a clothesline and roared a greeting at me, the typical Lladloh welcome.

"Who the heck are you?"

"I am Sadulsor Raleigh and I seek my father."

"Go look for him in a bicycle shop, you squeaky imbecile. You won't find him here. We are conducting a ritual of astounding complexity and importance. In fact we might utilise you as the sacrifice."

"Is a sacrifice necessary?" I asked.

He nodded. "Yes, yes! In fact we were going to employ Megan here for the task, but she's a very fine barmaid and we are loath to lose her when an alternative presents itself. You will do. Don't resist!"

This flabby threat was noisily approved by the others.

"What gives you the right?" I growled.

"Why, I am none other than Emyr James, landlord of this pub."

"And *that* gives you the right?"

"Yes, yes, of course. Doesn't it? If not then—"

"And I," gibbered another figure, "am Catrin Mucus; and this fellow is Phil the Liver; and that one is Iolo Machen."

"Dennistoun Homunculus is my name," said a gimp.

"Neifion Napcyn, that's me."

"Tee hee! They call me Pumpkin Hewin' they do!"

"Aye, and I'm Bigamy Bertha."

I grimaced and honked my horn. "I have no desire to know who any of you are. I seek only my father, my inventor."

"You wouldn't be referring to Mondaugen, would you?"

"Yes, I am! Is he among you?"

The man who resembled a skeleton clock now moved forward another tick and he rolled his large stained eyes at me. And then he spoke. He said six words in total but not as any ordinary man would say them. Each time he uttered one of the words, his head opened up like a lotus flower to reveal a smaller head inside; six blossoming heads mouthed a single sentence.

The sentence was: "I am Herr Doktor Karl Mondaugen!"

The sequence of shrinking heads was so disturbing in part because each head was rather beautiful, like that of a porcelain doll, a doll from some culture that was vaguely oriental but also childlike and brash.

But I merely said, "Atrocious!"

"He is such a good inventor he has invented himself!" chuckled Emyr James and his jowls made a horrid rustling sound.

"He is mechanical?" I gasped.

"Not entirely, no. But how did you get past the guard?"

"To be absolutely candid—"

"I didn't ask about Absolutely Candid, whoever he is, but about the sentinel, Perfectly Frank. Did you slaughter him?"

"He let me through because we might be brothers."

"It matters not. You shall die."

And the pallid crowd chuckled like feathers that tickle themselves, with very little conviction or mirth; and then Mondaugen's head, already smaller than a head had any right to be, blossomed again, and again, as it embarked on an occult chant designed to summon Ootoo from his cosmic tomb, from a hellish reality parallel to our own dimension, from one nightmare to another; and I watched in horror as that head grew smaller and smaller and smaller.

It was as if I was watching a traveller moving away over a landscape until he was just a speck, but one who had neglected to take the majority of his body with him on the journey, a ludicrous oversight!

"Namyllis Yrev Asaw t'Farcevol Enod Dnadias S'llanehw..."

The words were beyond endurance.

But they were effective. One moment the village square was empty.

The next it was filled... By Ootoo.

Yes, it is true. Ootoo appeared in person. One of the Old Ones. He was just a head, a massive head, a gruesome and monumental head. I'm sure he was more than that really, much more, intolerably more, but nothing else was visible. I could see only a head, a head so large it filled the square entire, pushing against the buildings that framed it, so that we had to retreat quickly to avoid contact with the glacially cold flesh of the lips and chin, which were at our end.

"That is Ootoo," said Emyr.

"I took that for granted," I answered boldly.

"And now we will give you to him; he will devour you and swallow you and digest you and excrete you and flush you."

"He has a clear agenda," I said.

"Yes; and why not? He is Ootoo, and what Ootoo wants, Ootoo gets, apart from on those occasions when he doesn't."

"He is a minor old one?"

"Perhaps, but what does that mean? Even the least significant old one is far older and far more of a 'one' than the most important gentleman in any armchair in any country on this planet. Ootoo he is. That is all you need to worry about. Ootoo and you. That is the nature of this scene."

"Why did you summon him?"

"To replenish our flagging spirits, to inject us with higher purpose. Can't you see how faded we are, like the ink of antique pages in rotting books? We are barely more substantial than fog. There is no fire in our veins. We are weary and indistinct and stale, going through the motions but never feeling or tasting anything. We care not if whole populations are annihilated now, that is none of our concern, but we do want to be alive again, to be three dimensional."

I felt an abrupt desire to be cruel, to strike back with words. "I doubt the fact of your fading away can ever be reversed."

"We shall see. Goodbye forever, boneshaker!"

"My name is Sadulsor..."

"Do you have a puncture, buffoon?"

"It is my mouth that hissed. My tyres are solid rubber that continually grows. No caltrap or pin can ever stop me in my tracks. This power was a gift of whoever made me, whether Mondaugen or not."

"Enjoy it for your remaining few seconds!"

Almost as if responding to a cue, Ootoo opened his mouth wide, jaw gaping to an even greater extreme than that of Perfectly Frank, so that the god resembled a serpent preparing to devour a serpent who already is gaping as wide as it can. And the gathering of spectral villagers moved closer to me. They intended to hurl me in the mouth. But I had no intention of being a victim. I would embrace my destiny in my own way, as I had always been fated to do.

I accelerated forwards, heading straight for that maw!

"What a rascal!" shouted Emyr.

"He's no son of mine," grated Mondaugen.

Ootoo's cakehole loomed huge.

And into it I went, leaping the bottom front teeth, landing on the tongue and hurtling down the throat, ducking my head to avoid striking it on that dangly thing with the name I can rarely rightly recall, the uvula or whatever, that pink and fleshy clapper like the teat of a oral udder that can be milked only for sounds. And then I was racing along the windpipe and still accelerating. And something peculiar began to happen. It stopped being organic anatomy.

It changed into something more geometric and hard. Into a labyrinth with an impossible number of diverging passages; and I selected my route at random, like a daytripper Theseus, my handlebars gleaming in the phosphorescent light of pulsing walls, seeking a Minotaur who was nothing but a case of indigestion somewhere in the endless turns of this gastric maze. And—

I came to a doorway but one without a door. It had merely a tattered tapestry covering it and I rode straight through it and found myself in a familiar office facing a man I already knew, who stood up abruptly from his chair, leaned on his desk and cleared his throat before speaking these words:

"Ootoo has already enrolled. It explains why our quota of monsters is filled forevermore. He plans to study theology."

"That's rather self-indulgent, don't you think?" I wheezed.

There was a pause and then at last...

The Dean of Lampeter University tugged his nose.

THE CAWL OF CTHULHU
Bob Lock

I was born and raised on the Gower and although I thought I knew much of its history I was surprised to hear of Granny Folvercat and her small house overlooking Rhossili Beach – which is on the southwestern tip of the peninsula. Gower is notorious for its rugged coastline, upon which a great many ships have met their doom and never reached port. Rhossili is one such place, and apart from the famous '*Dollar Ship*' which foundered with a princess's dowry of silver in the seventeenth century numerous other vessels have been lost, never to be seen again.

'The fire cleansed a great part of the common overlooking the beach. Mamgi Folvercat's long-house can be seen again. It's been some years since that place came to light. I saw it last, oh...' Tom Jenkins took a last gulp from his almost empty beer glass and eyed me enquiringly. I took the empty pint from him and waited for him to finish his sentence. 'Has to be about seventy years ago. I was a mere slip of a lad of thirty-something, I was.'

'Same again, Tom?' I asked, he nodded and gave me a toothless smile. Cathy shook her head at me when I ordered another round from her.

'You shouldn't encourage him, Bryn Evans, you should know better than that. He'll be shouting and singing next and you'll not be the one having to put him out when time is called. Even though he's over a hundred the old bastard can still kick up one hell of a fuss,' Cathy said. We'd known each other since primary school and whenever she added my surname to any conversation it was always to chastise me over something or other. I took the two pints from her, sipped a mouthful of mine and gave her a grin.

'One word from you Cathy and we'll all be running for the door, *you* know that, as well as *I* do.'

'You make me sound like a witch or harridan. Why are you even listening to the old fart?' she asked, 'you know all of his stories are bloody-well made up. If you were English I'd understand the fascination but *you* know the coast as much as he does.'

'True enough,' I said with a nod, 'but *I've* never heard of the wreck he spoke about or the Folvercat long-house. There can't be many ancient long-houses down on the beach and he reckons there was a stone circle in the back garden of it too. I've been down there hundreds of times and never seen it.'

'I've never seen it either and I've been down on the beach a lot more times than you. *You* were too busy gallivanting off to London to get that archaeology degree you found so important. Got fed up of the big city, did you?'

I didn't really want to get into it, how I'd had my heart broken in London and had come back to Wales to lick my wounds and lose myself, recuperating in the wilds of Gower, so I just shrugged.

'Got homesick – wanted a good pint – a good yarn and a good woman nagging at me. Where else was I supposed to come other than here?' I ducked as she threw the wet bar cloth at me and I took the beer back to our table. Tom smacked his lips at the sight of the pint and favoured me with a gummy smile.

'You're a good lad, Bryn, a good lad.'

'No problem Tom, can't let you get parched when telling me the story now can we?' I answered with a grin of my own and then Tom continued.

He told me that it seems no-one really remembered where or when Mamgi Folvercat, or Granny Folvercat as the English visitors used to call her, first appeared on Gower. But one thing was sure, she was a popular old woman, revered by the locals and visitors alike, and there had been many visitors. She lived alone but took in people for bed and breakfast during the holiday season and was always booked up. Her cottage was called '*Bullion Barn*'. It was supposedly built from the proceeds salvaged from a wreck that had gone down long before any of the locals could recall. Her breakfasts were renowned the peninsula over as being substantial and capable of keeping you going for most of the day. But her *pièce de résistance* was her cawl.

Dating back to the 14th century, cawl is unofficially recognized as the national dish of Wales. It's a broth made from leeks, vegetables and meat. Some use lamb, other use salted bacon or even beef. Mamgi's recipe was a secret.

'People used to queue from her house down onto the beach when she had a cauldron of cawl on the go,' Tom said with a glazed longing in his eyes and a dribble of spittle running down the side of his mouth. 'A lovely crust of bread and a chunk of cheese with it made it food for the gods.'

'I haven't had a decent cawl for years,' I answered.

'Aye, you haven't been in Wales for years, have you boyo?' Tom replied.

I nodded. 'True, but I'm back now. So, what happened to Mamgi Folvercat?' I asked. Tom shrugged his bony shoulders. 'No-one really knows. One day she was there, next day she was gone. Much like how she first appeared. Damn, how we missed her cawl. Someone once said she walked into the sea fully clothed and The Kraken took her up and ate her.'

I laughed. 'The Kraken? Like a sea monster?'

'Don't laugh about it man,' Tom said, all serious now.

'This coast has seen some strange things. A headless horseman galloping along the sands at midnight, the sea horse that swims off Falls Bay with a long neck and flowing mane and how do you think there are so many wrecks, eh?'

'Bad weather, hidden rocks, poor navigation?' I answered flippantly.

'Aye, those too, but when a beast from beneath the waves rears up and drags your ship down with tentacles the size of an oak, then weather, rocks and poor navigation are the least of your worries. That's what dragged the American here,'

Tom said and drained his glass again.

'Another, Tom?'

'Nay, lad,' he said shaking his head. 'I've put myself in a foul mood now talking about ghosties and ghoulies. I'm off home, Bryn.' I nodded and then asked.

'What American, Tom?'

'That Lovecraft bloke. He came the summer of '25 he did. Never liked him; drank shandy or light ale. I was but a youngster and could still drink him under the table. He wanted to see the Kraken he reckoned. Stayed at Mamgi's for a month or two,' he said and then tottered out and I watched him go with my mouth open in wonder.

'Good grief,' Cathy said as Tom closed the door behind him, 'What did you say to him, Bryn?'

'Nothing, was just talking about Mamgi's house on the beach,' I replied, 'I can't believe what he just said, he reckons H. P. Lovecraft was here in the summer of 1925. I never knew he even came to the UK let alone here. Tòm must be wrong.'

Cathy gave a little shiver. 'That bloody place,' her voice had a slight tremor in it. 'It's bloody haunted is that area. You don't want to be talking about Mamgi and you certainly *don't* want to be visiting the place.'

I shrugged. 'I wasn't going to, but *now* I'm interested. What do you mean it's haunted?'

'Strange lights around the old house,' she answered.

'Kids probably. That's what started the gorse fire I bet. Kids drinking and partying in the dark,' I said. 'What about Lovecraft, have you heard the rumour he was here?'

She shook her head. 'Never heard of him and no kids go there, ever. They've more sense than that. Not after the sixth one went missing.'

I looked at her. 'What? When was this?'

'First was years and years ago, too far back for me to know much about it. But there's been five more lately and the last was a couple of years back. Some kid who used to come down here surfing. From Newport he was, him and a bunch of his friends camped on the beach. Coppers said the kids reported they saw lights in the water and went to look, but didn't see anything. When they paddled their boards back to the beach one of them was missing. The kid was never found again but his board turned up. All shattered and broken with huge circular marks on it like something had sucked pieces out of it,' Cathy said and she shivered again.

'Creepy,' I said, 'want to come for a picnic on the beach tonight?'

'In your dreams Bryn Evans,' she replied and this time the wet bar cloth caught me full in the face.

My tent was a small pop-up type, no need for fiddling around, you just threw it on the ground and it erected itself. The sun had just gone down and I'd managed to find Mamgi's house whilst there was still enough light. Sure enough a big gorse fire had cleared a large area of the common just up from the beach. It had uncovered the huge stones set in a crude circle at the back of a dilapidated house whose walls had crumbled to tooth-like features rising up from the blackened earth. I camped within the circle, sheltered from the wind off the sea and beach by the ruined walls. Once ensconced in my tent and wrapped warmly up in my sleeping bag I booted up my iPad and started searching for Lovecraft's visit to Britain. Internet access was surprisingly good and I guessed it was due to the tall mobile-phone repeater mast I'd noticed in the pub's car-park. Twenty minutes of searching proved fruitless. Lovecraft was never mentioned as being in Britain and I imagined Tom must have been mistaken, although the date of 1925 would have been just before he had his story 'The Call of Cthulhu' published, so that, at least, seemed to make some sort of sense. I dialled up a colleague and a life-long fan of all things Lovecraftian back in London and a minute later we were Skyping.

'Not disturbing you Brad, am I?' I asked as he appeared on screen.

'Nope, wassup, Bryn?' he replied and looked closer at his screen. 'Where the hell are you?'

'In a tent on Rhossili beach, on the Gower peninsula back home in Wales.'

'What in the name of all the gods are you doing there?' he asked. He was a believer of all manner of weird and wonderful supernatural beings.

'You're going to love this,' I answered, 'I'm on the trail of Lovecraft and perhaps the location where he could have got his idea of Cthulhu from.'

'Have you been smoking wacky-baccy or something, mate?' he said with a laugh. 'You're on the wrong continent to be trailing Lovecraft.'

I explained to him what Tom has said and about all the rumours surrounding the area and he listened intently as the tale unfolded.

'I suppose it could be possible,' Brad admitted. 'He could have visited incognito. What's the spot like?'

'Creepy,' I answered. 'A lot of weird stuff's gone on around here over the years. I'm lying in a stone circle on a rocky piece of ground that's sticking into my arse.' I fidgeted and moved my sleeping bag to discover I'd pitched the tent on a protuberance of rock. 'Damn it, I'm going to have to move the bloody tent if I'm going to get any sleep tonight.'

'I don't know if I'd be able to sleep if I were there,' Brad said. 'Seems a bit of a scary place to me.'

'Nah,' I replied, 'I was born and bred down this part of the world. I've never encountered anything weirder than English visitors wanting ketchup with their cockles and laver-bread.'

'Yuck, how can you eat that? It's just boiled seaweed,' Brad replied.

'It's good for you, full of protein, iron and iodine.'

'Oh, well then, that makes all the difference, you need the iodine to counteract the radiation in your Chernobyl-infected lambs,' Brad suggested.

'That's a low blow,' I answered, 'I haven't seen a glow-in-the-dark one for years.'

'Take the iPad outside, let me have a look at the scenery,' Brad said.

I did so and scanned the heath behind me, which was now quite dark, and then followed the coastline down onto the beach and finally to the waves and the foreboding sea which looked dark and unwelcoming.

'Wait a sec, Bryn,' Brad interrupted. 'Did you see that?

Go back to the sea,' he said.

'See what?' I asked as I panned back and looked over the screen to the beach.

'Just beyond the waves, I saw a light,' he answered.

'I didn't see anything,' I replied and lowered the iPad as it was ruining my night sight. 'What did it look like?'

The answer was too quiet for me to hear properly and when I got Brad to repeat himself the blood chilled in my veins and it wasn't because the night was *that* chilly.

'It looked like a purplish light and seemed to be coming from beneath the waves,' he repeated and then the iPad bleeped once and switched itself off. The battery was drained.

It took me quite some time to drop off to sleep and more than once I thought to just pack up and go back to the little flat I'd hired temporarily until I decided on whether or not I was staying in Gower. But I finally succumbed and exhaustion dragged me down to an uneasy and dream-filled slumber. Whether it was the low chanting or the smell that awoke me I can't be quite sure but it only seemed I'd been sleeping for twenty minutes when my eyes flicked open and I checked the glowing dial on my watch. It was three a.m. and I'd been sleeping for almost four hours. I sniffed the air. The aroma was familiar. My mouth watered. I climbed out of my sleeping bag and unzipped the tent. The moon had risen and the circle of stones had turned to silver beneath its light. Beyond them shadows moved, and further out, a yellowish glow flickered. It looked like a camp-fire. I rubbed my tired eyes, groped for and found my boots and pulled them on. I started towards the yellow light as quietly as I could, the shadows seemed to flit around and follow me.

Whether it was my imagination or not, as I approached the fire, and the iron cauldron which was set upon it, the night appeared to grow darker. Even the shadows became more insidious as if they were trying to obliterate all traces of outside light and leave only the crackling flames as the single form of illumination in an otherwise void of nothingness. Finally all I could see was the dancing flames set within an infinity of black. Then something … or someone … stepped into the light.

'I warned you away Bryn Evans but you did not heed me.'

My eyes watered with the smoke from the fire, and the vision dressed in a dark purple robe was hard to discern, but the voice was unmistakable.

'Cathy?' I spluttered, 'you scared the crap out of me!'

'I warned you Bryn Evans,' she said again and she pulled the hood away from her head. As she did so the shadows around her resolved into people, people who were *not* people.

'Cathy, tell me this is some kind of bloody joke, you're beginning to worry me now!' I said and noted the tone of fear in my voice – and the horrendous damage to the people around her. Some were missing limbs; some had huge lumps of flesh torn from their mostly naked bodies. Yet all seemed to be surviving their wounds even as gore and blood oozed from them. All of them smiled at me which was perhaps the most frightening aspect of all.

'This is no joke, Bryn and you have no need to worry for He has chosen you and henceforth you will never fear again and you will live forever,' Cathy said and she produced a cleaver from beneath her robe. Its blade was stained dark red, almost black with old blood. 'The price will be a portion of your flesh for the cawl. All who pay the price get to serve Him and achieve immortality in doing so.'

Although I feared I knew the answer I could not stop myself asking the question.

'Him?' I said and that single word fell from my lips like a lump of clotted blood.'He who sleeps and dreams; He who is not dead which can eternal lie, and with strange aeons even death may die, Bryn. We all feed Him and He sleeps until the time is right, and we are worthy of opening the gate and keeping it open for Him and his kind to come through and bless us with His presence for eternity.'

'Oh dear lord,' I moaned, 'Cathy, you're talking about Cthulhu?'

She smiled and a madness gleamed purple in her eyes as she nodded and it took me a few moments to realise the purple was a reflection of something behind me.

'These are all the poor souls that have disappeared from around here?' I asked and waved a hand around the gathering.

'They were killed and made into cawl by Mamgi?'

'By my *grandmother*, yes Bryn. And *I* carry on the ritual. Now come, He awakens and your flesh must be prepared for Him.'

I stepped forward into the circle of light and she raised the cleaver high. My boot slammed into the cauldron and it tumbled towards Cathy spilling its sickly contents over her feet and she screamed and leapt back as the scalding liquid splashed. Vegetables, boiled limbs and lumps of flesh cascaded out to extinguish the flames. I turned and ran. The clearest path I had was directly onto the beach and that was the one I took. The huge beach of Rhossili is around three miles long and I was about halfway along it. The tide was in and waves were breaking nearby throwing phosphorous spume into the night. Behind me came the cries of anger from Cathy and her group of cadaverous followers, but overriding that sound was a muted rumble and finally a roar from out in the bay, and the sand before me began to reflect with a purplish glow. I lowered my head and put on a burst of speed just as something crashed into my back and I was lifted effortlessly into the air and pulled towards the water. As I turned my head I saw the monstrous thing rising from the breakers with enormous tentacles writhing in the air around it and with one great appendage attached to my back. I felt my clothing and skin begin to tear and I yelled out in pain and fear. The next moment I was plummeting towards the surf, and in a jumble of arms and legs I landed amidst the breakers. As something large crashed down next to me, groping and feeling for a purchase I managed to flounder onto the beach and sprinted inland. It was probably only minutes but it seemed like hours until I reached the road and managed to fumble the keys into my car and drive away at breakneck speed from the terror on the beach.

'You have no broken bones,' Doctor Ahmed said as he looked at my chart and then pulled up a chair next to my bed. I was in Singleton Hospital which was overlooking Swansea Bay and I had no idea how I got there.

'Do you remember the accident?' he asked.

'Accident?' I replied.

'Obviously you don't,' he said. 'Loss of memory is quite common after receiving a blow to the head such as the one you suffered.'

'What happened?' I asked.

'Your car left the road on the common on Gower, it's a write-off and you're lucky to get away with just cuts and bruises.'

'I don't remember much after leaving Rhossili,' I replied.

'Rhossili?' the doctor frowned. 'Couldn't have been Rhossili, perhaps you mean Port Eynon the one before it?'

'No, it was Rhossili,' I repeated. 'Why?'

'Oh, just that the BBC News said Rhossili was closed for a day or two because they'd found an unexploded mine on the beach and no-one has been allowed access.'

I laid in bed dropping in and out of sleep for the best part of the day and in the waking moments ran through what had happened that night. I began to doubt that it had ever happened at all and perhaps it *had* been the blow to my head. That evening Dr. Ahmed called in to see me again. I was sitting up in bed and looking at the evening sky over Swansea Bay. My thoughts were a million miles away.

'How are you feeling this evening?' he asked me as I turned to him.

'Fine,' I replied. 'Can't wait to get up and about. Lying in bed has made my back ache.'

'You can sit in a chair, you know?' he replied and he gave me a hand to get out of bed. We walked over to the window and I sat facing into the room. 'Your back will improve in time; you're bound to have it aching for a while though with bruises like that. I've certainly never seen anything like them.'

I suddenly felt chilly and I shivered involuntarily. 'Bruises?' I asked.

'Of course,' he replied with a nod. 'You couldn't have seen them. They're almost circular, about six to eight inches across and the centre looks almost bite-like; you've lost a little flesh from those parts. It's no wonder your back is aching.'

I suddenly felt queasy and was glad I was sitting down. I looked up at him but he was staring over my head out of the window. Behind him two hospital workers wheeled in a trolley with the evening meals upon it. Dr. Ahmed frowned, shook his head slightly and then smiled when he saw the food being served.

'Ah, enjoy your tea Mr. Evans; this is one of the rare Welsh dishes that *I* particularly like too. It's not as spicy as my Arabian *Tabakh Rohoo* lamb stew but your cawl is certainly an enjoyable dish.'

I swallowed so noisily I imagined the whole room heard it. He looked at me quizzically and then his attention was drawn to the window again and I felt sure I saw a flare of purple reflect in his eyes and although I was tempted to turn around and look out to sea myself I refrained from doing so and wondered if it was too late to catch the last train back to London.

PILGRIMAGE
Mark Howard Jones

"Here is a platform alteration. The 16.53 to Swansea will now leave from Platform Zero. Passengers for this service should make their way to the new platform."

I could have kicked someone! Two heavy cases to be carried down one set of steps, along a corridor and up another set and all with just three minutes before the train was due to leave. And why Platform Zero? I was sure that was for local services only and didn't even connect to the main line. No doubt we'd be told it was an error as soon as we got there.

The train was already pulling in as I arrived at the top of the platform steps, sweating and panting. As the doors clunked open, disembarking passengers streamed past either side of me, almost pushing me back down the steps at one point.

I joined a group of people clustered around one door, waiting to climb aboard as soon as the stream of those getting off had ceased.

In the few seconds I was standing there, I became aware of a group gathered behind me. I glanced over my shoulder and saw four identically dressed men with pale skin. They were all quite short, almost stunted, and all seemed to be staring at the back of my head.

They made an odd giggling noise among themselves and, as soon as I turned away, I felt a finger poke the back of my head. I wheeled angrily. "You cheeky little f—," I began, before noticing a mother with her young daughter standing behind the men.

My temper had been on a hair-trigger since my wife's 'disappearance' almost a year ago; I'd thought it was a struggle I was winning. So I contented myself with glaring at the odd group before picking up my cases and getting on the train. The giggling idiots followed me and, as soon as I'd stowed my cases and found my seat, they trotted past me, carrying on an excited conversation in an unrecognisable language.

Only when I ran my hand over the back of my head did I discover the source of their mirth. I made a disgusted noise to myself and visited the toilet to remove the pigeon's gift from my hair. Two paper towels later, the job was done. At least my hair is still thick enough that I didn't feel it, I mused, then got my comb out to repair any stylistic damage.

I settled back down into my seat and fished around in my pocket for the scrap of a paper on which I'd written the train times. A 55-minute journey to Swansea, several minutes of which had already been used up, lay ahead of me. Then a tedious half-hour wait for my connection to Milford Haven. I should still have enough time to pop out for a beer or two after settling into the guest house I'd booked.

I'd have to turn my attention to finding somewhere more permanent to stay in the evenings, after my shift at the refinery was over.

I felt guilty about leaving Rose with my sister but I needed this job; I didn't want a life that was just memories. And I couldn't look after a five-year-old at the same time. Once I was established in my new place, I'd come and fetch her. Besides, Rose was settled in school now and Bethan was more than happy to look after her.

Cardiff was left behind as the rural scenery of the Vale of Glamorgan rushed past the train window in a green blur and I closed my eyes, hoping to doze off for a bit.

I was jolted awake at Bridgend when, despite its smoothness, the inertia of the train stopping tugged at my inner ear. The bustle of people finding their seats subsided after a few minutes and the train pulled out again.

I managed to doze once more and only woke as the train

passed the uneven sunlit hillocks of Kenfig Burrows. I imagined walking across them to the unseen sea beyond, and closed my eyes as the train sped past the huge steelworks just before Port Talbot station.

There weren't that many people waiting to get on at the station. One figure hung back from the others as they crowded around the train doors. The man with dark skin had the air of someone who rarely hurried, as if that was something for lesser mortals. He had no cases or luggage of any kind with him. My eyes were drawn to him because he stood very erect; something that is unusual these days.

Suddenly, he raised his hand and held it out towards the train. Something sat on the palm of his hand. The object was a dull golden colour. He was several yards away and, from this distance, it was difficult to make out exactly what it was – it looked at one moment like the discoloured heart of a large animal, then a second or so later it seemed like an obscure abstract sculpture. No, no ... it was some sort of squat animal perching on his palm as if about to leap at me. Presently I had to look away as the effort began to give me a pain behind my eyes.

The man pocketed the odd object as he approached the train, walking past my window in his progress towards the First Class carriages. He was very well dressed and from a distance I'd assumed from his skin colour that he was either African or from the Caribbean. But now I could see he had more Caucasian features. Yet his skin was the blackest I'd ever seen on a man, more like carved stone than flesh, while his eyes had a peculiar amber hue more common to domestic cats than people. As he passed out of sight, I puzzled at his origins.

The sounds of doors slamming along the length of the train signalled our readiness to depart. I was sure that something within the train had changed; maybe it was that the temperature had crept up slightly but it felt more to me as if the air itself had thickened, becoming less fluid than before.

It was more difficult to move my head, it seemed to me. I wondered for a second or two if I was having a stroke. Finally I did manage to turn my head and gazed out of the window at my side as the train left the platform behind.

Against the grey sky, the steel plant had been transformed into something remarkable and unfamiliar. I'd passed it hundreds of times but it had never looked like this before.

I had paid no attention to it as the train had pulled into the station, in fact I'd closed my eyes, but now I couldn't tear my gaze away from it. The towers were now impossibly tall and had taken several huge steps toward the station, threatening to crash down onto it. The entire plant had been transformed into a single building of enormous proportions. Parts of it hung in the air, seemingly not attached to anything else, while other sections of the building seemed to fold in upon themselves before opening out again, like impossible flowers blossoming.

The industrial grey of the steelworks had become a livid orange that was interspersed with a bronze pouring down its surface in a waterfall of bright fire before the ground swallowed it up, becoming tainted with the darkening hue. Strange things appeared to be moving around the building. I struggled to see what they might be but the train sped away too quickly, for which I should have been grateful.

On the horizon, strange shapes marched out to sea. Or were they coming this way? Once they had been cranes but I couldn't begin to guess what they were now.

The trees we passed had been transformed, too. They seemed soft, as if it would be impossible to climb them. Their leaves – if that's what they were – moved unnaturally to the urging of a breeze that could not exist.

I decided I needed some air. Maybe that would clear my head; I was clearly hallucinating. As the doors slid open to allow me into the vestibule that connected my carriage to the next, I saw a middle-aged woman with greying hair crawling on the floor. She was being thrown about by the motion of the train and was saying over and over "Oh Lord, help me. Oh Lord, help me." I leant down to help her up but she jerked away and rolled herself into a ball against the wall, her fingers curling over the lip of the inset litter bin. She kept her face turned away and continued her unending prayer. I got the brief impression that there was something missing from her face.

PILGRIMAGE

Slightly offended that my offer of help had been spurned, I decided to leave her to the train guard and went to a door to let the window down. The breeze whipped into my face and within a few minutes I was able to convince myself that I felt better.

Turning to return to my seat, I noticed a man lurching towards me down the aisle. He was blocking my way so I stood and waited for him to pass. As he approached I noticed that his eyes seemed oddly glazed. His step was more uncertain than could be explained merely by the motion of the train. Eventually he made it as far as the door, which opened automatically to allow him through.

"There's plague on board ... it's plag—" He held out a bottle of water and a partly unwrapped sandwich to me. I stepped back, watching in disbelief as both items were swallowed in seconds by a white fungal growth. The items dried and disintegrated before my eyes.

I forced myself to look away as something told me his hands and then the rest of him would soon suffer the same fate. Covering my mouth and nose for fear of breathing in anything, I began to run up the carriage. Behind me came a noise like a vacuum cleaner pipe becoming clogged.

I plunged through the door into the next carriage, the familiar hiss and clunk of the door calming my nerves only slightly.

Those announcements were always urging passengers to 'contact a member of the train crew' if we saw a suspicious package. This was a damned sight worse than a suspicious package, so that's what I was going to do. The buffet car was my best bet, I thought. But it was at least three carriages away.

As the train lurched around a bend, almost threatening to tip over it seemed to me, a bird, or something very like it, smashed into the window. It seemed to crawl along the glass for a few moments, a huge thing with black feathers and large claws and *teeth*. I turned my head away quickly but curiosity forced me to look back. It had teeth, I was sure of it. They could clearly be seen within its misshapen beak, attempting to gnaw at the glass. The animal clung on desperately before it was torn away by the wind as the train picked up speed. A woman sitting nearby had also seen the monstrosity and turned to look at me with terrified eyes. "What was it?" she asked in a very small voice, shrunken by fear. I shook my head and continued towards the buffet car, not wanting to think about what I'd seen.

I paused at the carriage end. Only one more to go now. As I prepared to sway and lurch along the aisle once more a woman came staggering towards me. I reversed out through the doors, which opened reluctantly behind me so that she almost ended up careering onto me. She uttered just one sound, regular and low, over and over again. "Eeeeee. Eeeeee. Eeeeee."

I peered into her eyes. At first I thought she wore trick contact lenses, but then I realised that it couldn't be the case. Her irises and pupils had been replaced by tiny clock dials, the minute and hour hands showing just one minute to midnight while the second hand raced towards the vertical.

Her face flushed a dozen vivid colours as her mind melted inside its bone prison. "Gypped!" she gasped, then slowly disappeared, as if eaten alive by her surroundings. Disbelievingly, I stepped forward and waved my hands through the space where she'd been like an idiot child. There was nothing.

I struggled to remain calm, noticing that my mouth was incredibly dry, my heart almost rearing up in my chest. I had to get to the train guard. They had to stop this, even if it meant halting between stations and getting all the passengers to safety. I had no idea what was threatening us but something was terribly wrong.

Pressing on, I entered the final carriage. I could see the counter of the buffet car through the door at the far end. I had just passed the second row of seats when the air was torn open by the sound of every phone in the carriage ringing at once. All around me people fumbled in clothing and bags, trying to find the devices and shut them off. Some had them already in their hands but seemed unable to do anything but stare at them as in a trance.

Covering my ears with both hands, I pressed on down the carriage as quickly as I could. In front of me, a man stood up, rummaging in his coat. Quickly I pushed against the top of his seat and balanced on the arm rest of the one on the other side of the aisle. I had to get out of there.

The few seconds that I'd been forced to uncover my ears had allowed the sound to slice into my head. A dull ache had begun in the very centre of my head as if my blood was being pushed into places it wasn't supposed to go. It seemed to grow worse with every second as I struggled forward. Now it was as if a hundred tiny claws were scrabbling in my skull in a frenzied bid to break open the bone and get out, while the air pressed in on my eardrums as if I'd suddenly plunged into deep water.

The phones continued to ring as people struggled with buttons and swiftly removed batteries to try and silence them. Nothing seemed to work. Children had begun to wail. A woman was screaming. Another had begun forcing a knitting needle into her own ear.

I passed the four strange men I had seen on the platform. Out of the whole carriage, they seemed the only ones unaffected by the terrible assault on the nerves. In fact, they seemed delighted by the sonic chaos around them, seated around a table and exchanging grins.

What had begun as a cacophony of various ringtones and snatches of music had now changed into one sound, high and insistent. The phones had all begun to sing, if that was the word. The almost absurd diversity had blended into one keening crescendo, an otherworldly fluting that worked its way brutally into the brain of everyone who heard it.

By now I was nearly at the end of the carriage. I was sweating and in pain, almost blind with something bordering on fear. Finally, I was near enough. Pushing a woman and child out of the way, I lunged at the door and, not waiting for the automatic mechanism to open it, clawed at one edge. I forced my muscles to obey me and pull the sliding door aside, almost falling into the vestibule beyond. Crawling across the space dividing the two carriages, I reached up to the handle of the toilet door. I yanked down on it and leaned against it at the same time.

As I tumbled inside, I yelled out in relief. Then I stopped

in mild panic. I'd given voice to a word I'd never heard before. It was a strange word but one I somehow knew meant a form of redemption or safety, maybe a rescue of sorts.

I clambered to my feet and forced the toilet door closed behind me. Now, at last, I could no longer hear the music. I ran cold water over my hands and splashed it on my face, trying to forget the altogether alien word that my tongue had uttered.

Drying my face in a handful of a paper towels, I stood with my back to the wall and tried to remember who I was. As my eyes re-focused, words began to write themselves across the opposite wall; a sort of sordid Biblical imitation. The characters were bizarre and unfamiliar, totally unintelligible. I had a sense that they were incredibly old, though they appeared far too complex and sophisticated for any ancient race that I was aware of. A form of long lost Arabic, perhaps? The words "I was, I am, I will be" insinuated themselves into my thoughts.

I had no idea what the phrase meant. Yet another puzzle to contend with. I sighed heavily and pulled open the toilet door. As I stepped towards the link between carriages the train leapt sideways, sending me sprawling into the buffet car. I had got here at last, though I hadn't intended to arrive face down.

Clambering to my feet, I was astonished, though not surprised, to come face-to-face with the dark-skinned man I had seen earlier on the platform. Somehow it seemed right that he was here. I didn't know who or what he was but this was obviously his base, from where he had transformed an ordinary train into a hurtling nightmare; his own kingdom of pain.

Taking my courage in my hands, I pulled myself up to my full height and, aiming at a commanding tone, I addressed him. "What do you know about what's going on on this train? One man said something about a plague ..."

At first I thought the dark man was going to deny any knowledge of the strange events. But instead he said softly: "The only plague here is that of knowledge. But that is easily dealt with."

Behind the man, sitting on the buffet side-counter, I saw

the object he had held in his hand when I'd first seen him. Even this close, it was difficult to make out exactly what it was. It looked like something vaguely animal but there was an element of chaos about it, as if all its parts were in a constant state of change. As I looked at it I realised that it was changing, slowly and hypnotically, as new forms sprang forth from it just as others sank away into the main body.

I looked back at the man, puzzled, pointing at the object. For a few moments he said nothing, but when he spoke once more his words sounded like some bizarre religious pamphlet.

"You are a pilgrim. You seek forgiveness, confirmation, redemption. It is all available to you." As he spoke, I noticed the depths of his dark eyes seemed as if they were moving, as if they were not eyes at all but merely portals into an unknown place where all hope had been extinguished, all memories devoured.

I looked around me. The familiar colours and shapes had all begun to change. Tones of an undiscovered spectrum crept into the usual subdued reds and blues of the train's mundane livery, transforming it into a living masterpiece.

"Does it please you to see the world in its true form at last?"

"But ..." I began. I stopped, looking around me with revulsion, then glared at the dark stranger. "This can't be how the world really is," I said, defiantly.

He nodded, lowering his eyes. "Oh yes. Oh yes. This is your world ..." he said softly.

Behind the dark stranger stood a line of people at the buffet counter. Their skin seemed waxen, their eyes as dead as cold ash. Two of them turned their shrunken mouths to me and, with huge effort, tried to move their leaden lips and granite tongues.

The dark-skinned man saw my eyes darting from one to the other. "Do not be concerned about them. They will be joining us soon," he said. I didn't know what he meant but the statement made me fear for my own safety. Did I now look like them? I searched around for a window or some other reflective surface.

Stepping over to the nearest window, I saw that the

surface had become dull and had a texture almost like that of fur. It was completely opaque. Instead I ran my hands over my face; I could detect no changes but how could I be sure? My senses were betraying me, seemingly changing their function as I struggled to maintain my balance within the speeding prison.

I clenched my fist, digging my nails into my palms. I spoke slowly, deliberately. "What is happening here?"

"You should prepare to meet your maker." The words fell from his dark lips as if made of stone.

This time the answer was obvious to me, despite the throbbing in my head; I wasn't buying into any religious crap. "I don't believe in God!"

"Neither does your maker. At least not in *that* God!" He was worryingly close to me now. "I can assure you that the old gods are dead – the older gods have returned!"

I thumped my hand against the wall in anger, expecting it to hurt. Instead the soft wall absorbed my brutality with a dull thud that seemed to last most of the day. "Who the hell *are* you?!" I demanded.

"My name is Nyarlathotep."

"Nye who?" The first part of his name definitely sounded Welsh but the last part was a bit of a puzzle. He didn't answer but simply stood staring at me with a slight grin on his face, as if staring down at an interesting insect, knowing its doom was not far off.

"Nye who?" Again he simply stood there, as if deliberately testing my patience; provoking me passively from behind his frozen face.

"I said 'Nye who'?" I was almost yelling now. This time he smiled, showing shockingly white teeth that contrasted starkly with his ebony skin. He shook his head from side to side, openly mocking me.

I could no longer contain my anger and lunged at the man. But the distance between us opened up until it was vast, uncrossable. I felt dizzy, as if I was looking down from a great height and my body was rebelling against it. My anger was useless, I realised. I tried to think clearly and struck on the idea of performing an everyday task, to try and pull myself back from the brink. My hands felt too heavy to be of any use so I decided to ask a question. A normal, everyday question.

"How long before we reach ...?" I had meant to say Swansea but my mouth formed a series of sounds and syllables that seemed to get tangled within each other. I uttered a a a word that seemed impossible, that my mind could not grasp and that my memory rejected.

The dark man smiled. "Soon," he whispered in a booming voice.

I staggered back out into the carriage vestibule and leant my forehead against the cool of the glass. I panted like a thirsty dog on a baking hot day.

The train roared through a small station at enormous speed. Several filth-caked things could be glimpsed reeling and flopping on the platform in the semi-darkness.

As the train rounded a bend, the silver sliver of the River Tawe visible below us, it barely slowed at all, the metal wheels screeching in protest. As the distance was eaten up, I caught a glimpse of the station ahead through the window. It had changed. I knew it would have. It had grown enormously and towered ahead of us, like something made from splinters of diseased glass or broken pieces of bad, old dreams.

I braced myself against the door, closing my eyes against the vertiginous speed. My insides felt as though they were being torn out. Screams reached me from elsewhere in the train.

The train finally halted with a sound like a hundred huge hammers pounding on a steel skull.

I felt the stranger's hand on my elbow. It was ice cold. "Come," he said. I opened my eyes and looked at him. The door at our side folded or melted – or something between the two – but suddenly it was no longer there. I stepped onto the platform, glad to be still for just a moment. A long, precious moment when I thought, stupidly, that everything might be all right.

A sound like a hundred corrugated metals huts being torn apart by a huge machine came from behind me. The appalling sound drew my attention and I glanced over my shoulder. The train was crumbling in upon itself like a dried-up old leaf.

I turned to the strange, dark man, who was now a yard or two ahead of me. "What about the other passengers?"

"Surely it's traditional to bring offerings on a pilgrimage?" he said, coldly.

I knew then that I wouldn't be returning from this place, this city that was no longer a city but merely wore the face of one. I prayed to God – whichever god was listening in this unearthly place – that my daughter would be safe.

I couldn't pretend to be sad to leave behind a world so rotten that it had allowed me to do the things I had. But I did grieve for little Rose, growing up without her father. Then again, maybe she'd be better off out of my poisonous clutches; maybe she'd grow up clean.

Several dark shapes lay, groping eyelessly along the platform across from where I stood. The dark stranger turned to me and, in a voice that turned the air chill, said "Fellow pilgrims."

The sky above the station had turned bright copper, the unclean light seeping down the station walls and bleeding onto the platforms. It was just inches from my feet now. But they felt like lead, unable to move even an inch.

When the light reached me, a shock ran through my body, stealing my breath away and making me sweat as if I was fevered. My innards clenched. It passed in a few seconds; I became aware of the taste of vomit in my mouth and a warm dribble of semen trickling down my leg.

Behind me I could hear his voice; it came from the bottom of a million-mile deep well. "This is an old land – I was here before, long ago. But this time I will create it anew. It begins now …"

A keening sound like the wind forcing itself into the narrow spaces between buildings filled the station. My feet were forced forward, moving me to the end of the platform alongside all the misshapen creatures. God only knew what our future held … or if we had any sort of future at all.

Slowly, heavily my feet inched forward. Though my face remained impassive, deep within me the remains of my soul screamed as the station exit opened like a huge maw, ready to swallow me.

SONG OF SUMMONING
Brian Willis

PREFATORY NOTE – When Professor Colin Vernon was compiling his authoritative critical biography of the (hitherto largely forgotten) English composer Edward Raphael Holt (1764-1805), it was, as he noted, a source of considerable frustration for him that, in a career otherwise meticulously recorded by way of diaries and letters, one period in Holt's life remained a mystery; the period covering Holt's residence in Wales between September 1801 and his 'breakdown' (to use the modern parlance) and subsequent return to London in early 1802.

Since the publication of Professor Vernon's book ('Edward Raphael Holt; The Genius Muted', Oxford University Press, 2007), there has been a resurgence of interest in this lost, forlorn figure of the English Romantic movement. A season of his music was programmed last year at the Barbican; a documentary on his life was broadcast on BBC4; and there is talk that Sir Simon Rattle is to record at least one of his symphonies.

This is all a far cry from the indifference with which Holt's music was received by his contemporaries. Music in Britain was in a largely fallow state during this period; after the glory days of Purcell and Handel (an adopted Englishman), little of any lasting merit was being composed, and the majority of what found favour were Baroque pastiches. Only a few obscure composers in this drab, conservative England were daring to wade into the dangerous seas of Enlightenment and Romanticism, to go alongside Holt's contemporary Beethoven and others on 'the Continent' in celebrating a new freedom of thought, of Reason, and of Art.

Poets at this time were, of course, less constrained; and it was the friendship of one of England's greatest poets, William Blake (himself a figure ignored and even reviled in his time), that inspired Holt to some of his greatest work. The manuscript of Holt's second string quartet (1789) is dedicated to Blake.

It is likely that Holt's fame would have grown (particularly if he had ever been able to take his music across Europe, where it may have found a more receptive audience) were it not for his tragically early death at the age of just 40, and for the bizarre – and thus far unexplained – events in Wales which drove him to madness.

Only six months ago, however, a puzzling document was found tucked away in a collection of the miscellaneous papers of Holt's brother-in-law, the poet Walter Deakin (it was Deakin and his wife, Holt's sister Edith, who cared for the composer in his last years, at least until he was considered too dangerous to be kept at home, and was confined to the infamous Bethlehem – or Bedlam – asylum). The Deakins had relocated to Massachusetts after Holt's death, and many years later Deakin's descendants donated his papers to the library at Miskatonic University. Although no firm provenance has been established – the possibility of fakery cannot be discounted, as Miskatonic has a certain arcane reputation for the discovery in its archives of 'historical documents' of dubious pedigree – a preliminary linguistic analysis, comparing the writing style to that in documents incontestably authored by Holt, has produced a result of roughly 75% probability that they were indeed written by Edward Holt. A handwriting analysis came to a similar conclusion, the levels of doubt occasioned by the variable grammar and almost childlike penmanship in the latter part of the text.

This material is therefore printed here for the first time. The strangeness of the subject matter may jar, but in the context of Holt's mental deterioration, and his prior tendency to experience what we would now call 'auditory hallucinations' (in the form of a music which he described as "so sweet and ethereal a sound that it can only come from the Seraphim themselves!"), it may have a certain consistency.

I have sent copies of this text to Professor Vernon for comment. That was two months ago. Since then, he has been most uncharacteristically reluctant to speak to me, or to anyone else, on

SONG OF SUMMONING

the subject of Edward Holt.

— B.W.

SEPT. 16th, 1801

I have been in Wales for scarcely a day, but already I begin to feel some of the melancholy that has fallen upon me of late begin to lift. It may be that the air of London has grown too stale to tolerate (although I am assured by friends that it is no better nor worse than it ever was), but in this place so far from the dirt and stench and corruption of the city, where even the rain seems to be a cleansing, almost *joyous* thing, I feel my mind once more begin to soar and sing.

Ah, William! How absurd now seems your devotion to that monster, London! More like Sodom does it appear now, further than ever from becoming the New Jerusalem…

I have taken up residence in a cottage found for me by my old friend and school-fellow Nathaniel Evans (now organist and choir-master at St Woolas Cathedral, in Newport, not far distant) in a small village called Brynteg, close to the old Roman fortress town of Caerleon. The village's name means 'fair hill', and my mind instantly pictured a domain of the 'fair folk', said by ancient lore to once populate these isles. So far, alas, I have encountered not one of these elusive creatures, but the beauty of my surroundings makes me think that there is no place in this land where they are more likely to be seen. And I have been here, as I said, only a day, so I must be patient!

A short walk takes me from the cottage to the village, and on the way I pass a most picturesque lake, called by the locals Llyn-yr-Eglwys, or 'Church Lake' (Here, I must record my indebtedness to the pastor of Brynteg, the Reverend Gwilym Morgan, whom I met and conversed with for some time today upon my arrival, for his advice on Welsh spelling and pronunciation). He is also, I believe, an expert on local folklore, so I am resolved to ask him tomorrow, since he has invited me to visit with him tomorrow, about the origin of the lake's name, since I can detect no trace of any such building – or habitation of any kind – on the lakeside.

Now, as I prepare to lay down my pen, I see that night

begins to fall. To my joy, I begin to hear the sweet music which has been withheld from me for so long in London. I am too weary to try and capture it now; but I feel sure it will still be there in the morning, and for many mornings yet to come.

SEPT. 17th

On first awakening at dawn, my immediate impulse was to try and capture on paper some of that music which had been playing within my mind for most of the night, even to the extent of underscoring my dreams (which, it is interesting to relate, featured the nearby lake as its centrepiece, though in what precise context I cannot recall). Only after three hours of futile effort, scribbling on paper and pawing discordantly upon the pianoforte (found for me and transported here in time for my arrival by my most loyal friend Nathaniel), did I concede defeat, for that morning at least, and repaired back to my bed to spend a further hour in grim, bitter indolence.

Only the sudden recollection that I was due at the home of Reverend Morgan that afternoon stirred me from my torpor. The sunlight radiating upon the house warmed my spirits, and as I washed, shaved and dressed in fresh clothes, a little of the spring returned to my step.

My path to the village took me once more past Llyn-yr-Eglwys, and as I sauntered around its perimeter, I found my pace, almost involuntarily, slow and bring me to a halt, gazing across that preternaturally still mere at the mist-mantled hills opposite. Until that moment, my thoughts had been governed by the beauty and serenity of my surroundings, but as I stood there, another sensation washed over me; an intimation of something intangibly *wrong* with what I beheld. I can only liken the feeling to that which one, such as myself, who is graced with perfect pitch, feels when a single misplaced note on a single instrument in an orchestra disrupts the perfection of a performance.

Am I too fanciful to connect my sensations at that moment with my dream of the previous night? It would please me to say that it is so.

Departing from that place in some confusion, it took me twenty minutes more (walking at a much brisker pace than had marked the earlier part of my sojourn) to reach the Reverend Morgan's cottage. I was welcomed with great delight, and much bustling courtesy (displacing a cat from an armchair so I could sit, imploring someone to make tea, calling for his daughter to come and meet me) by that jovial gentleman, and felt no different than if I was a friend of many years acquaintance come to call.

With the tea served (by his housekeeper, an apparently long-suffering woman who smiled at me politely, but whom the Reverend neglected to introduce), and a plate of the local bread, or *tesion lap,* as it is called, placed before us, my host's daughter, Olwen, made her appearance. A most delightful girl, of some twenty-one years, with good conversation and deportment, promised in marriage (the Reverend proudly informed me, no doubt to forestall any amorous inclinations on my part) to the son of a wealthy wool trader in Newport. Modestly, she told me she played a little upon the clavichord, and with my encouragement she played a short local air (the name of which escapes me, but it was perfectly pleasant), well enough not to offend my sensibilities too greatly. Having taken my appreciation of her skills with great gratitude, she left us both to our discussions, saying she had business in the village.

Charming as she was, I welcomed her departure. I wished to question her father on the local folklore, particularly with regard to the lake. Without telling him of my peculiar sensations at the lakeside, I asked him if he knew of any stories appertaining to Llyn-yr-Eglwys.

"There is a legend in these parts," he said, after a moment's thought, "that the lake was once dry land, a valley. In that valley stood a city ruled over by a wicked prince whose iniquities and vices were so great that the bishop at that time took him to task. The prince was so furious that he had the bishop slain in his own church. Before the bishop died, however, he cursed the land, and set the church bell ringing. Now, the church was said to have been built upon the site of a holy well, and at the sound of the bell the well overflowed like the waters of the Red Sea rushing back upon Pharaoh, and drowned the land, and everyone in it."

He gave a chuckle. "It is attested by many in the village – usually after the inn has closed its doors – that the church bell still rings, deep in the waters of the lake, and can sometimes still be heard."

"Is there any factual basis to this tale?" I asked. Something in my countenance must have disturbed him, for he sat forward and looked at me intently.

"My dear young fellow," he said, patting my hand, "it is merely a legend, a folk-tale. In every part of Wales... every part of Britain, for all I know... you will find similar stories. Why are you so concerned about our lake? You have been here for only a day."

I could give him no answer. My visit to the lake earlier had broken my dream of the previous night, stirred up feelings and strange fears to which I could as yet give no voice. As I sit here and write, hours after I left the Reverend's cottage (as quickly as politeness would allow) those forebodings are still with me.

On my way back here, I took pains to find an alternate route. One that did not take me past the lake.

SEPT. 18th

A low, clinging mist, which drenches to the skin all those who venture abroad in it, has settled in upon the area. At mid-day, the light was scarcely bright enough to be able to make out words upon a page, even when reading by a window, and I was compelled to light candles in order to continue my work. How strange it is, that one's spirits can be so overthrown in the short space of a day, and by so mean and commonplace a thing as the weather! I endeavoured to remain active, however, and placed myself with steely determination before the pianoforte, only to endure another fruitless afternoon's attempt at composition. The music in my mind is dull, muffled; and no breath of inspiration stirs in me with which to blow away the clouds which smother it... smother ME...

I can endure this wretchedness no longer. I still have some

laudanum, purchased in London, and I can only hope that this black humour will disperse after some hours of repose, and I will awake invigorated.

SEPT. 19th

I awoke to the first light of dawn (if such a pale, drab glow can be truly worthy of the name), my mind in a maelstrom of fear and confusion, at first unwilling to trust that what my eyes were seeing was the real world, and not a continuation of the ghastliness that I visited in my dreams, a ghastliness that, even now, I am loath to recall. Indeed, even if I were less unwilling to do so, I do not believe that my descriptive powers are adequate to the task; what follows is the nearest semblance of cohesion that I can impose upon what I, in experiencing them, perceived as little more than a chaotic gallery of abomination.

As I pitched downward into my laudanum-induced slumber, I heard, to my initial joy, the Angelic Music once more, and so clear and sharp that I felt that its creators were all around me, guarding me as surely as mothers implore them to protect their infants during the hours of darkness. That feeling of serene ecstasy bore me ever deeper, through warm caverns of peace and stillness and absence of mind...

But abruptly the music changed. It became strangely discordant, even as I thought myself to be closer than ever to its source. It seemed that I was hearing the music *truly,* in its purest form, for the first time.

I had been deceived. Ensnared.

And then my eyes were opened.

I found myself on a dry plain, beneath a sky that boiled with clouds the colour of spilled blood. In my nostrils was the stink of decay and corruption, and looking about me I saw the carcasses and sand-scoured bones of beasts that my imagination defied me to identify; beasts which walked (or perhaps, *slithered*) upon no Earth that was familiar to me.

Upon the plain, some miles distant but still towering upward into the crimson sky, was a structure unlike any I had ever beheld. It pointed at the unruly heavens like the blasphemous finger of some accusing Titan, ebon-black and jagged, and at its apex burned a beacon of sickly green flame. I knew it to be an intelligently designed and constructed artefact, and not a natural formation, but quite how I knew it to be so I cannot explain, for the thing appeared from its features to be an organic thing, not unlike the giant termite nests of Africa and the Americas of which I have heard. Perhaps it was the strange way in which the light reflected off the surface, revealing angles and geometries too regular... and yet *inhuman*... to be vegetable matter or some freak of geology.

And then the music... my beloved, 'angelic' music, now revealed as a perverted and damned thing... changed once more. It rose to a raging shriek that set my skull ringing fit to burst. I tried to open my mouth to scream, but my incorporeal body in this place would not obey me. My vision was directed upwards, to the red sky, and I saw huge shapes begin to detach from the great tower and rise upwards in ever-widening spirals until they filled the air like locusts. I could discern little detail, for the main bulk of their bodies seemed to be naught but formless blobs, but their wings were large and almost transparent, like unto those of a moth.

All the time, singing. My angels.

Then, motion upon the floor of that wasteland caught my attention. From the base of the tower, other shapes were emerging; wingless, their motion ungainly and yet embodying a powerful purpose. They were rushing towards me, a great herd of these ill-formed beasts spreading outwards in all directions. Even with such a distance between us, their terror was palpable.

They were seeking escape... but from what?

The sky roared. The crescendo of the 'angel's' song had been reached. And, as I watched, so at the very centre of that whirling mass, a hole, like some awful black sun, appeared to open, and with their songs still ringing across the land, all the flying creatures were sucked into that abyss in the sky and, in only a few scant moments, were gone.

With a final, terrible percussion, the black sun vanished.

And I then heard the piteous wail of the creatures left behind.

Something else, also; in the distance, beyond the mountain range which curved around the periphery of the plain, a low rumbling could be felt, and was just reaching the limits of hearing. It was from this, I knew, that the benighted monstrosities closing in on me were fleeing.

And then I saw it. Crashing through the mountains was a tumult of water, a wave higher and more dreadful than any I could have thought possible. What had instigated this deluge, I could not tell, but the torrent raced towards the great tower at astonishing speed, sweeping up the dust and debris of this dry land before it.

The beasts now emitted a mournful howl that seemed to signify that they knew the futility of their attempts at escape. They seemed, as one, to slow, and what had sounded like a cacophony now became almost harmonised, as if in their last moments they had resolved to sing themselves into eternity.

And as they did so, I felt their eyes – eyes in faces which I could not as yet see clearly – fasten upon me.

They were singing for me.

And I knew for what terrible purpose they did so.

I tried to implore them not to choose me for this task, to let the cup pass to another, but they were implacable. In me lay their only hope for salvation.

And their salvation would damn me.

The wave of water struck like a hammer blow of Neptune then, cutting short their voices, engulfing them and crushing them into the depths to be forgotten and silenced for ever. In the last moments, I saw their hideous, unformed faces, like the smooth features of some embryonic demon, mouths open in song and supplication…

I awoke weeping. I think that in my first moments upon awakening, my memory of those creatures' message to me was still hideously clear, but as I lay, bathed in sweat and feeling as disconsolate and as far from my fellow man as if I were on another world, the meaning of that message slipped from the forefront of my mind. Now, I can give no words to it at all; and yet, in the depths of my soul, somehow I fear that the message remains, and will guide my hands to do God knows what actions.

Can I pray to be forgiven for a sin that I have not yet committed? That I cannot even define? What hope can one such as I—

(The subsequent paragraph is rendered illegible, as if Holt had second thoughts about what he had written. There are no further entries for the period of the 20th through to the 22nd of September — B.W.)

SEPT. 23rd

I have had time to consider my experience (can a dream be truly called an 'experience'?) of a few nights ago. What seems most terrible and fearful in the immediate aftermath of such a thing can, upon more sober and reasoned reflection, be seen as little more than the product of a disordered mind. I know that my dear friend Blake trusts in the potency and veracity of visions, but I have always been of a more sceptical disposition in these matters, and thus I have come to certain conclusions about what I 'saw'.

Firstly, the pressures upon me in my latter days in London had been great; debtors had been pursuing me, my publisher was anxious for new work (long promised, and much overdue), and my drinking and use of laudanum had been much increased. My escape to the relative peace of Wales had done nothing to relieve my sorrows, and may in fact have exacerbated them, by giving me the time and solitude to brood. Furthermore, taking the laudanum last night, when my imagination had been already disordered by my new surroundings, must surely have contributed, as had my failure to eat anything of any real substance since I have arrived here.

I have composed nothing in these last few days. So obsessed have I become at my futile pursuit of the elusive music of my 'angels' that I have neglected all else. I must return to work. Even if it means that I block up my ears, like Odysseus, to their siren call, I must force myself to compose, in order that the capacity does not atrophy within me for want of use.

But I am so very weary. I have slept little. Every time my eyes close in slumber, echoes of that fearful dream return to me, and even though I now know it to be the mere product of an over-stimulated imagination, the terror of it still jolts me awake.

More, I believe that parts of the dream are becoming more vivid; it seems that the faces of the creatures that I saw are as clear as my own, seen in a flawless glass. Blanched skin; black, lidless eyes; organs that pulse repugnantly within their translucent forms; and a cluster of protrusions on the lower part of the face that wave and entwine as if possessed of independent life. I see them, borne on the wave that will ere long crush them into the depths of a new-born ocean, reach for me with long, many-jointed limbs mounted with fearsome claws, reach for me in desperation… Enough. I shall write no more this night.

SEPT 24th

The capacity of the human soul to renew itself once more became an astonishment to me. By putting aside all the hideous fancies which have of late beset me, and concentrating upon a pursuit most directly in opposition to that which has been upon my mind (I had embarked upon the composition of a series of variations of that same Welsh folk song which Miss Olwen Morgan played for me, when I visited upon her and her father), I raised myself this morning from the 'slough of Despond', and once more felt ready to face the world.

The oppressive weather which has hung over these mountains has now lifted, and this afternoon I walked to the village, where I partook of a simple lunch of bread, cheese and ale at the inn. I find the Welsh to be, in general, a most courteous and hospitable people, yet I am not unaware of how curious a specimen they must perceive me to be. As I sat beside the fire in the inn, I heard the landlord and some of his 'regulars' speaking in low tones at the bar, in Welsh; and although I have as yet only the most scant of understanding of this tongue, I several times heard the word *Saesneg* (meaning 'English') used, as well as the word *gwallgof* (note; check spelling and pronunciation – as well as meaning – with

Reverend Morgan).

In late afternoon, I set out once more for my lodging-place, but decided – emboldened, I think, by my new-found rationality and ease of mind – to take the least circuitous route, along the edge of Llyn-yr-Eglwys.

At first glance, the lake was much as I had seen it on that first day; calm, tranquil even. But the longer I stood there, the more I was unable to shed the feeling that this appearance of peace was only a mask, concealing something altogether more unsettling, more... *malign.* I realised, with the force of epiphany, that although there had been all day a vigorous breeze moving across the land, the waters were as untouched by it as if they were made of iron. Even on the lakeside, I could feel the wind upon my face, weaving mischievous fingers through my hair; and yet on the face of the waters – nothing. The lake contented itself to its passive, imperturbable state, reflecting sky, sun and cloud as perfectly as if that reflection were a continuation of heaven itself.

And hard upon this, another revelation; it was not the wind alone which left this place undisturbed. Even at this period of the year, there should have been some sign of bird or animal life, either upon it or at its edge. But of such life was there none, not even the movement just below the surface of fish or amphibian.

All about me, the trees hung silent. Nothing dared to sing.

A most curious calm enveloped me, an absence of all emotion, care or joy, as if I had entered a place entirely beyond the reach of the temporal world. If I stayed there, at that spot (it seemed to me), I could remain ageless, rooted, part of the landscape, akin to one of those great ancient stone monoliths that some say are the petrified forms of knights of long-ago, perhaps even great Arthur himself.

Curious to discover the consequences, however, I stepped closer to the water's edge and, kneeling in the reeds, stretched forth one hand to touch the water's surface.

Instantly, a shock of great power, like unto a lightning-charge, leapt through me and convulsed my entire body.

Visions. Blanched flesh, black pearl eyes. Talons. The aeons of cold time. Division. Lives incomplete, unrealised.

We must return. We must be complete. You must assist us, summon us, guide us through the Door…

I must have fallen in a faint. When I regained my senses, the sun was dipping behind the western hills, and my body shivered and ached terribly. Through dimmed eyes, I could see the lake, still so apparently demure and dormant. Darkness was slipping lower, and I knew that my sanity would never recover if I remained long in this place, so I dragged my unwilling form upright and set my feet for home.

When at last I arrived, I secured the door behind me with great diligence, and, having lighted as many lamps and candles as I could to ward off the oppressive darkness, fell into my chair in a terrible fugue. I think I remained unmoving in that chair for at least an hour.

It was as I finally stood, in order that I might come to my writing-desk to record the aforesaid experiences, that I felt a weight in the pocket of my coat. Reaching in, I found a long, wooden tube, approximately eighteen inches long. Holes were drilled along its length, as well as an opening at one end and a mouthpiece at the other; obviously a simple wind instrument of some kind.

Besides the holes, a parade of stick-figures, *man-like* figures, engaged in a pursuit the precise object of which I would prefer not to speculate.

I had no recollection of picking up this 'pipe', nor, I think, would I have kept it if my wits had been fully in my possession. I hastily put it in a desk drawer, to examine more fully in the light of day (and of Reason).

SEPT 25th

This morning, I examined the 'flute' (it seems most convenient to refer to it thus) in detail. In daylight, it seems a much less mysterious thing than it did last night, but it offers up no more ready answers than my previous perusal, except to say that its maker must have been a person of no mean skill, since the cutting of the wood seems to have been effected with very great precision (none of the clumsy scratches upon the wood that a more slipshod artisan would have left), and even the apparently primitive stick-figures along the side are executed with some care and deliberation.

Perhaps I can reach some conclusions by playing upon the flute. I will undertake such an endeavour this afternoon.

The same, later—

As I sit to record my observations, I notice with some surprise that my labours have cost me no less than *five hours!* Time has sped past me as I sought to bring music from the flute. I was successful in this – but oh, what music it was!

Unfamiliar as I am, on anything more than a rudimentary level, with the playing of woodwind instruments, I felt straight away that this instrument was not fashioned with an ordinary player in mind. The finger-holes were positioned too far apart to be bridged by the fingers of a hand of regular proportion, and the mouthpiece was of a most unorthodox shape.

That said, I found myself capable, with some effort, of bringing forth a few notes. Only slowly, as my skill grew, did I realise that the sound I was producing *was familiar to me.* Played by musicians more adept than myself (perhaps naturally so) but nevertheless unmistakeable.

It was the sound that I have heard in my mind for as far back as I can recall. My 'music of the Angels'.

Now it is clear to me why all my previous efforts to replicate that music were doomed to futility – such beauty can only be conveyed using the instruments of its original creators!

Surely the hand of some divine Sponsor is at work here. Only such a force could have directed me to this place, at this time, to make this most glorious discovery! The true nature of my terrible, vivid dreams and forebodings is now clear to me; some agent of the Devil put them into my mind in order to prevent me from attaining this Revelation of the divine, the *visionary* work which the Almighty has decreed for me.

I offer up a prayer of thanks to my God, and dedicate my life to Him, and to the work of bringing to man the music of the Seraphim. "Holy, Holy, Holy."

Amen.

A seven day gap in the journal now ensues.

OCT 2nd

I have had little time in the last week to record my activities, so only now at last do I take up my pen once more.

In truth, little worthy of note has occurred to me in the mundane, temporal world. All that I have undertaken has been conducted within the confines of these four walls; more to the point, within the confines of this skull!

It took me some time to master the art of playing that Angelic flute. My fingers ached from being stretched into (for me) un-natural contortions in order to reach notes. My breath was likewise found wanting, though this had much to do with my own lack of practice in the piper's art; until I had perfected the necessary breath control, I oft-times found myself faint from the exertion.

Nevertheless I have (once I had made some amendments to the customary system of notation to compensate for the unearthly nature of the music being recorded) filled sheet after sheet with the music which flows through me, as if at last I had one of its creators at my shoulder, urging me on to greater and greater achievement (though I must have a care; I am not exempt from the sin of pride).

But the dreams remain. Evidently my demonic foe has not yet given up all hope of thwarting the Divine Will. They are subtly altered, however; I still find myself on that bleak, unyielding plain, gazing up at the tower. There is no sound, no music, no sign of the creatures or any other form of life within the citadel. I feel as if I am being silently watched, studied.

Although for what, I cannot conceive.

From this point onward, the entries become irregular, and are undated (though context suggests they were written over the space of 2-3 weeks subsequent to the last dated entry).

I have not eaten, nor slept, in two days. Body and soul cry out for rest, for ease and sustenance, but what little sleep I find is plagued with visions of that nightmarish plain (always silent and still, poised on the brink of that final oblivion), and all food and drink tastes of naught but ashes. The most I can tolerate is a little water which I take from the rain barrel outside, but even this tastes sour and corrupt to me.

I wander the house, playing upon the flute, the patterns and harmonies which I previously heard in the music now flattened out, almost atonal. Sometimes it seems I am not alone here, that there is another presence in this house; it darts along corridors and past doorways, always at the periphery of my vision, but is gone before I can look fully upon it. Do even the shadows conspire against me?

But I am reluctant to leave this house. A dread of the sky has come upon me, for I fear to look up and see the heavens replaced with the bloody tumult of my dreams, and then to see that obscene black sun gape above me and disgorge upon the earth…

The shadows are massing at my back. They will not reveal themselves to me, but I know who they are. They are the Damned, the ones left behind to die upon the Earth when their 'angelic' kindred found the means to escape the inevitable doom that would wipe them from history. They still remain, in the timeless spaces of the world, half-corporeal things, denied the rapturous transfiguration of the Winged Ones, shambling through dreams and shadows to work their influence upon mortal men, upon ME, to use me as their cat's-paw and send them to the starry abode of those who abandoned them… or to bring back those ones back, to rule once more upon this world… or to have their vengeance upon them…

I do not know! God help me, but their purpose, their minds, the sound-magic with which they exert their hold over my soul and body and the very universe itself… I cannot comprehend it!

But it is not my place to comprehend. I must simply 'do'. The music burns my mind now. They call the tune, and I must play.

I slept, and I dreamed of the citadel.

I dreamed that I stood before them, massed there within their nest, and played. They hissed, and writhed with delight.

Their time was at hand.

I awoke, beside the lake. The flute was in my hands. I was barefoot, wet, cold and shivering.

Looking at those moon-haunted, imperturbable waters, I tried to recall how I had got here; but of memory was there none. An irrational rage rose in me; were *they* laughing at me? Was the lake? The *moon* itself?

I gazed down at the flute in my hand, and considered for a moment – a *long* moment – simply throwing the accursed thing into the lake, as I should have done at the very beginning.

Such thoughts were cleared from my mind when I caught sight of the grass and reeds around me. There was no sign of my footprints in the damp grass, or anywhere close by. There was, however, a long trail of flattened grass leading to my current location, from the direction of the cottage.

I had *crawled* here. On my belly, like a serpent.

The music will re-unite them. Scattered across the Cosmos, they await the signal – the music unheard on Earth in aeons – to once more be whole.

I see the truth now. Not two species, two races, but one. They separated the godlike portions of their being and sent it away to an unknown star, to await the day when their earth-bound counterparts would find one (such as myself) able to summon them home.

I have been prepared for this my whole life. This is the purpose of my existence, my music.

The return of the Dark Gods. The obliteration of mankind.

They make me dance. It amuses them to make me dance. The stick-figures on the side of the flute? They are me. Dancing to their tune.

i crawl to the lake again and again to their sunken citadel below the waters, below time

the taste of blood they have not tasted blood in millennia

so sweet

the night given shape

they wait beyond the door the song so clear

(The final entry, which may come from any time between late December 1801 and early January 1802, is spotted with a substance which could be blood. No analysis on the document has, as yet, been undertaken. — B.W.)

POSTSCRIPT – A few weeks after the initial (and much commented upon, not all of it kindly) publication of these papers, I received a letter from Mr Kenneth Lewis, local historian and folklorist of the village of Brynteg, for some time engaged upon an edition of the collected sermons and writings of Reverend John Vaughan, grandson of Gwilym Morgan, who had followed in his grandfather's footsteps by becoming pastor of Brynteg.

In Morgan's papers, he found a passage which, after reading the 'Holt Breakdown Diaries' (as they became known), he felt he should pass on to me. Reverend Gwilym Morgan had, according to his grandson, been witness to 'a most curious and disturbing event'

He writes;—

> "In the last weeks of 1801, into early January 1802, the village was much alarmed by a series of night-time attacks upon the flocks of local farmers. A wild beast, perhaps a wolf, was thought to be ravaging the countryside; livestock were being slaughtered and their partially devoured carcasses strewn about the fields. A group of locals, led by Ifor Beynon (who had suffered the greatest losses) set up a hunting party to try and bring the beast down.
>
> "One night, it was reported that a creature of some unknown type had been spotted along the shores of Llyn-yr-Eglwys,

and a large hunting party convened, with lanterns, cudgels, and even a pistol or two, to make chase. My grandfather, despite his great age (and my mother's protestations), was not to be left out, and joined with them to troop down to the lake.

"For an hour, they prowled, halloo-ing to each other through the dark woods beside the lake, until at last the cry went up, that it had been located!

"Close on midnight, in the circle of lanterns at the lake's edge, a group of men stood swinging their lanterns to try and get a better view of something that lurked in he darkness at the base of the tree-line. My grandfather could not make out what it was, but said it appeared to be seeking a way to get past the men and to the water.

"Then, all at once, the creature darted from cover and charged at them, knocking one man over in the process It had almost reached the water when Ifor Beynon discharged his pistol. The shot merely grazed the creature across the forehead, but it was enough to stun it long enough for a half-dozen or so of the village's sturdiest men folk to wrestle it into submission.

"Then there was a cry. 'By God,' says Dafydd Rees, 'it's a man!'

"And to be sure, he was right. My grandfather came forward, and looked upon the face of the wretched specimen, and had to squint because of the poor light, and the blood upon the man's face, and his own failing eyesight, but (he told me, many years later) he knew the man.

"Though he would not name the man he saw, and took the secret with him to his grave (and made all the others there that night swear on the Bible to do the same), a rumour floated down to me from another source that an Englishman of some renown had been staying in the area, had gone violently insane, and been taken back to an asylum in London.

"And also this; one of those present that night said that, before being taken down by the pistol shot, the 'creature' threw something resembling a stick out into the deep water..."

Mr Lewis related to me one last anecdote; a boy, in the 1860s, claimed to have been led to the lakeside by 'fairy music', and found, in the reeds, a strange 'pipe' or 'whistle', which seemed to want him to 'play upon it'.

Frightened, the boy threw the pipe into the lake, and ran home.

THE NECRONOMICON
Charles Black

At first I did not recognise the man on my doorstep, and had half a mind to pretend to be out. Yet, when he glanced briefly upwards, there was something about his face that stirred my memory. Not so much the features, but rather the man's superior expression, that seemed somehow familiar.

He was a little under six feet in height, and had thinning, sandy-coloured hair. He was carrying a brown leather briefcase.

As I observed the caller surreptitiously from the upstairs window, I saw him look at his watch impatiently. And although I anticipated he would only turn out to be a door to door salesman, I hurried downstairs to open the door.

Before I could speak, he boomed out a greeting, "Hello Durward."

At once I recognised the distinctive, deep, Welsh voice. "My Goodness, Rhys-Morgan!" I said in amazement.

"Yes it is," he said, granting me the briefest of smiles.

"Well, this is a surprise," I said, as we shook hands. For it had been many years since I had last seen, or even spoken with Gwyn Rhys-Morgan.

"I hope you don't mind me turning up like this, all unannounced," he said, as I ushered him into the house.

"Not at all," I replied. "Come on in."

"In here, is it?" he said, ignoring the door to the sitting room, and selecting the door to my library.

"Unerring as usual, Gwyn."

"Of course," he said, entering the room.

"Make yourself comfortable," I invited, taking his overcoat, though my visitor declined my offer to take his briefcase.

Instead of seating himself in one of the pair of armchairs, Rhys-Morgan began studying the books that lined the shelves – that came as no surprise.

I was about to ask what he would have to drink, but my guest pre-empted me. "I'll have a scotch please, Durward."

"It must be nearly fifteen years," I said, handing him his drink. And I still found it annoying how he would call me 'Durward' after the Walter Scott novel rather than use my name.

"Yes it must," he replied.

We had been at Cambridge together. Although we weren't exactly good friends, it was through our shared interest in rare books that we knew each other.

A silence ensued, as Rhys-Morgan scanned the titles of my books. I was about to comment on how I had obtained a particular volume, but he held up a hand as if to stop me.

Awkwardly I waited until he had finished his silent perusal.

"An impressive collection," he said at last, taking a seat.

"Thank you," I said, as I seated myself.

"I suppose you're wondering what's brought me to your door after all this time." Once again he had pre-empted my question.

"Well, yes, I was actually."

"I have it."

"It?" I queried.

"It." Rhys-Morgan nodded.

I was puzzled. "I don't understand, Gwyn."

What he said next astounded me.

"*The Necronomicon*," he stated simply.

I gasped audibly. "*The Necronomicon*?"

The Necronomicon: The book of the mad Arab, Abdul Alhazred. A legendary book of blasphemous and cosmic revelations. That utmost grail for seekers of occult knowledge, and of many bibliophiles. And Rhys-Morgan's taste had always leaned towards the outré.

"Yes."

"But how? Where did you find it?"

"My search was long, and often frustrating, but I always remained persistent. I began with libraries, and museums, antiquarian book shops, eventually widening my search.

"Do you know, the British Museum had the audacity to deny me access to their rare books collection. I wonder if they had some inkling of my intention to make their copy my own?" Rhys-Morgan paused, apparently brooding.

"It was the same story again and again, at the Bibliotheque Nationale in Paris, and in Rome, and Cairo. Miskatonic University in America as well. Have you ever been to America, Durward?"

I shook my head.

Rhys-Morgan frowned. "Terrible place. You'd do well to avoid it," he advised.

"In so many places, either I was refused permission to view the book, or my enquiries met with denials that the book even existed."

I found what Rhys-Morgan said next to be somewhat far-fetched.

"I have travelled the world, not just in body, but in astral form. My quest has taken me to many strange places and I have witnessed even stranger things."

"How extraordinary."

"You think I'm being fanciful don't you, Durward?"

"Well, I'm not sure I follow you exactly, Gwyn."

"It's all right." He waved a hand dismissively. "How could you know? You have spent your life blissfully ignorant of the true nature of the world around us."

I didn't know what to say to that, so I said nothing.

"From major cities of the world to rundown and decrepit towns in rural New England. I have infiltrated cults of diabolic purpose, and searched the tombs of necromancers, that lie in ghoul-haunted graveyards."

Fanciful was the word all right.

"But all this was without success. Yet I did not give up.

Then after hunting high and low, and far and wide, I finally tracked down a copy. Would you believe that after all my travels, I located one in an obscure part of Gloucestershire, of all places?"

"However did you afford it? You must have come into a great deal of money, or had one of those incredible pieces of luck where you found it going for a song."

"It was in the possession of a man called James Goodman. I managed to make him part with it."

"Congratulations, Gwyn. I must say I'm honoured that you should think to inform me after all this time," I said.

I refilled our glasses, and asked, "But have you read it?" At the same time eager that he had, but also afraid that he might have done so. For *The Necronomicon* has a dark reputation. It is said that its contents can drive a man insane.

"Oh yes, I have read it. My mind reeled at the cosmic revelations, the unholy and unimaginable truths it contains. Yes, I have drank deep of its forbidden knowledge."

Despite what Rhys-Morgan said, I wanted to see it for myself. I eyed his briefcase. "And you have it with you now," a statement rather than a question.

He nodded.

"May I see it?"

"Of course." He rose, and took his briefcase to my desk. I joined him, and he opened the case, and took out the fabled *Necronomicon*.

It was a large volume – a folio, I estimated at least a thousand pages in length, and bound in dark black leather.

"Incredible."

With a trembling hand I caressed the cover, then carefully opened the book. "My God, Gwyn! This becomes even more incredible. I had anticipated John Dee's translation – but this is remarkable."

Rhys-Morgan had managed to obtain the Italian printing of 1501, printed in black letter gothic type.

"Yes," he replied, "I too thought that there were no longer any copies of this edition extant. However, I suspect that it is not the original binding."

I marvelled at the pages of text – the fantastic legends that were the ravings of a man thought insane.

Here and there were marginal notes written by numerous different hands. There were stains that might well have been blood. Some pages were torn and a few entirely missing – not surprising considering the book's great age.

I puzzled over strange cosmological diagrams. Wondered at perplexing rituals of sorcery and a blasphemous religion. And shuddered at illustrations of monstrous creatures labelled: *From Life*.

"Wonderful!" I declared. My thoughts were covetous. "How much do you want for it?" I asked,

"Oh, it's not for sale."

I sighed. It was the answer I'd expected.

"I doubt whether you'd be prepared to pay the price anyway," he said cryptically.

Then after a moment he said, "At the back of the book you will find there is a list of names, such as is sometimes found in a family bible."

I turned towards the rear of the book and found the list.

The first name was Anotonio Carlucci with a set of dates 1501-1505. Gian Mollisimo 1505-1519 was next. Then Ricardo Del Vascao, 1519; followed by Fernando Diaz 1519-1535. After him was John Maltravers, 1535-1554.

"It's impossible that these are dates of birth and death," I said. "They must be dates of ownership of the book."

Another thought occurred to me, "These names, they appear to be written all in the same hand."

Rhys-Morgan nodded.

"For someone to have traced the ownership of the book back through its history is a remarkable act of scholarship. But you are not responsible?"

Rhys-Morgan shook his head. "No."

I read further down the list. Raschid Ibn Malik caught my eye. His dates read 1609-1759. "But that's impossible, a hundred and fifty years."

Rhys-Morgan smiled at my bewildered expression.

"Imagine, how I impatiently turned the pages to find the end of the list, eager to add my name and thus confirm my rightful ownership.

"Then imagine how my mind reeled when I saw beneath the name of James Goodman, already written in that same red ink, my own name."

"What? But that's impossible."

"Is it?"

I turned to the end of the list. Sure enough below James Goodman 1934-1936, was Gwyn Rhys-Morgan 1936-.

"Well then perhaps Goodman, knowing he was going to sell the book to you, had already appended your name to the list"

"That's just it. You see, Durward; Goodman wouldn't sell. No matter how much I offered him he refused."

"Then how?"

"I killed him."

"You did what?" I don't know which stunned me more: the fact that Rhys-Morgan had killed a man, or the casual way that he had admitted it.

"You do see that I had to? Don't you, Durward? I had to have it, it was rightfully mine."

I smiled and nodded, thinking it wise not to antagonise him.

Rhys-Morgan continued, "You said that the dates were dates of ownership rather than dates of birth and death. You were partly right. Ownership yes, but also year of death."

I frowned. "Are you sure?"

"I did do some research of my own, and found out about some of the names on the list."

"And?"

Rhys-Morgan began picking out names from the list. "Ricardo Del Vascao, tortured to death by the Inquisition in 1519. Agnes Lamprey was burnt at the stake in 1603. In 1759 Raschid Ibn Malik was stoned. In 1793 Louis Rocheteau was—"

I interrupted, "Let me guess, another victim of the Reign of Terror?"

"Perhaps. It's not clear what happened exactly. Although what is certain, is that he was torn to pieces, various parts of his body were found all over Paris."

Rhys-Morgan continued his morbid recitation, "Matthew

Horne was killed in the Indian Mutiny of 1857—"

"Well, lots of people were killed during the Indian Mutiny," I pointed out.

"Yes, but Horne's body was found covered in curious bite marks and completely drained of blood." Rhys-Morgan smiled. "Josiah Wellsby had it after him – he committed suicide in 1859. Every one of them died in the latter year listed."

"What about Goodman? How did he come to have the book?" I consulted the list, the name above Goodman's was Victor Goodman.

"His father," Rhys-Morgan said. "He inherited it from his father."

"There you are then, he died in bed, after living to a ripe old age," I said, with an optimism I did not really feel.

"Actually, you are almost correct, Goodman senior did die in bed. Goodman boasted that he smothered his father with a pillow. His father got it during the war, looted it off a German he killed." Rhys-Morgan pointed to the name above Victor Goodman's: Pieter Mueller.

Suddenly Rhys-Morgan began to laugh wildly. "Don't you get it yet, Durward?"

"Calm down, Gwyn," I urged. "What ever do you mean?"

"What does the title *Necronomicon* actually mean?" he asked.

"The title's in Greek," I said. "It's the name given to the book by its translator, Theodorus Philetas. "Mentally I translated the title. "It means… My God!"

"Yes, Durward, imagine how I felt reading my name in *The Book of Dead Names*."

It was not long after his visit that the police arrested Rhys-Morgan following an anonymous tip-off.

He was found guilty of James Goodman's murder. And when the death penalty was carried out, the year marking his demise, and the end of his period of ownership of *The Necronomicon*, appeared written by that unknown hand, in that same red ink.

And the name of the book's new owner duly appeared

beneath his.

Rhys-Morgan was wrong; I am prepared to pay the price – eventually.

You see, I believe that somewhere in its pages Raschid Ibn Malik found the secret of a preternaturally long life, and I shall find it too.

Quentin Richley,
April 1938.

Addendum: Quentin Richley died in August 1940, one of the many casualties of the Second World War.

UN-DHU-MILUHK WOULD
(IF HE COULD)
Liam Davies

Early December, 1990

To begin, it is winter in the Valleys, and it is a moonless, starless night in the village. The blanket of night spreads out and up over the beached whales of the surrounding hills. Gorse skeletons rustle to the melody of the evening breeze and beneath the snoozing township of Treorchy, Elder God, Un-dhu-miluhk writhes between blanket seams of coal, on the cusp of wakefulness. Above his snug, gaseous head, the houses are as still as churches along the frosted edges of the hunched high street and all the people are sleeping too, slumbering deep in the snug-still, still breathing town.

Hush, the babies are sleeping now, and the butcher, baker, punter, bookmaker; the callous-handed handymen, the farmers, fishmongers, and clacking-tongued pensioners, and, perhaps the most of important of all, the new breed of ground-digging men and their protective canaries, intent on pulling tar-black rocks from the ground in the nearby colliery to keep mankind marching to the beat of the electricity drum. Power.

Young girls lie, tangle-limbed beneath gossamer, marshmallowed duvets, gliding through dreams adorned with hoop earrings and charm bracelets to the melody of Un-dhu-miluhk's soothing, sonorous snoring that rumbles the

Rhondda and rocks their beds, as if they sleep within the lilting snuggeries of babies. The boys are dreaming naughty, of copping fondles and unhooking brassieres behind the bottle bins round the back of the Co-op. The cotton bud sheep sleep in the fields, the cows in the byres and the dogs in the concrete-cool back yards; and the cats either nap in the nooked ledges, or slink, weaving and wandering along the terraced roofs.

And in spite of His sleeping, from the bottom of the big-pit, Un-dhu-miluhk can hear the frost crystals forming, the blind houses breathing, the coal miners dreaming. And as He sleeps, the songs of His dreams drift through the transoms of the dreamers above him, drawing the miners ever deeper in their pursuit of coal, coaxing them down with their picks and their shovels and their drills, ever deeper towards His goal, of seeping out through the mine caves and, CROESO, out into the Rhondda atmosphere. He dreams of the black and folded night above him, fast, and slow, asleep. He dreams of moving, circling Treorchy, wider and wider, swooping invisibly over Treherbert and Pontygwaith, ever increasing in arcs over the valleys so He can become embalmed in Her scent upon the gilded winds and find her once again. Even through the mists of dreams, She is as clear as a window onto his own gaseous soul: Rhu-thmar-duhk, the eternal concubine, Widow of the Western Winds. He dreams of her. He dreams of that one night when they came into contact. Her curves, her soft, weighty breasts, the mouths that adorn every inch of her abdomen, bosom, neck and face, each capable of the most exquisite song. Every inch of her bewitched His being. All thoughts of dominion, destruction and rule disappeared. There was only Her. He was nought but a spent abstraction of his forebear, Cthulhu, nought but a passing of gas from the vile passage of a worthier deity, for Un-dhu-miluhk was wasted, diluted by love. He dreams of his vaporous tendrils, clinging to Rhu-thmar-duhk's wrists and ankles, pulling her pale, furred limbs apart; he dreams of creating a sensuous breeze with his own being and letting it lick gently against the folds of her sex; he dreams of her orgasm, the eternal wailing winds from each of her bodily mouths, the earthly storms that

followed, that scattered his airy form on the gales, his blind
drift across the earthly realm, until he settled, amidst peat and
grass, spent, barely there, a million years ago; He allowed
sediment and trees to form a blanket above him, and as the
earth folded him into its embrace, he fell into a satisfying,
dream-filled sleep.

Dreams.

Dear Rhu-thmar-duhk, my love
There are bonds more literal than ours,
And singing hills and summer doves
And valleys bejewelled with flowers.

So love, why don't you fly to me?
On winds that eddy and bole
Above this nation, of daffs, Taffs and leeks
To my bed, twixt two seams of coal.

Should you come, and come you should
I'd enflame you with song and with verse
There we'd canoodle, our romance would bud
And I'd wed you for better, for worse.

Oh mouthy madam, malevolent vessel
I'm gaseous and flaccid and hurting
But you know too well, from that time when we wrestled
We spark like Taylor and Burton.

I could say it's love, but it's sex too, you see?
If I weren't just a vapour, I'd be your bit of rough
But it's not going to happen - ach y fi,
But Un-dhu-miluhk would if he could.

And the dream expands; an imagined exchange:

UN-DHU-MILUHK

    Rhu-thmar-duhk!

RHU-THMAR-DUHK

Un-dhu-miluhk!

UN-DHU-MILUHK

I am the spawn of an Elder God and am mad with love. I love you more than all the hot Welsh cakes in Wales, fresh off the griddle and mellow with butter; than the oil cloth, the dragon, the stove pipe hat, Tiger Bay, Tom, Shirley and Bonnie; than elaborate amourous spoons, Chippy Alley, collieries and Porthgain crab. I have risen from these malnourished, tar-black depths to claim you once again. Throw away your frilly bed-socks and flannelette house-coat. I will warm the sheets like a Breville. I will coax puckering from your many lips about your whole body, like a sink plunger... like an owl, I could have *the wit to woo* you?

RHU-THMAR-DUHK

I am the eternal concubine. Widow of the Western Winds. And I will sing you a song using all of my expectant mouths, all of my honeyed gullets, to help your mind and body to rest. I will warm your cockles with both fire and fur, so your cockles are both firmed and fired...

UN-DHU-MILUHK

Rhuth, Rhuth, before the miners, those blind mice, wake me and I come to find you once again, will you say

RHU-THMAR-DUHK

Yes, Un, yes, yes, yes...

UN-DHU-MILUHK

And all the celestial bells of the universe shall ring for our wedding.

And now, still, in spite all dreams, it is chill in the town; it is night in the Methodist chapel, hymning in the pews and piles of bible-black bibles; it is night in the bingo hall, as quiet as an empty card; it is night in Howard Street, snaking silent, with sponges-inside-socks on its paws, past curtained collectable toys, paint by numbers, potted lava bread, love-spoons on nails, wooden dressers, Denbeighshire display pots and the blinking red eye of neddying VCR players.

He dreams. It is night. Time passes. Time passes. Time passes.

They're coming closer, the miners are, slowly digging him out. Any day now. Time passes. More time passes. Dawn comes, day dies, night falls; dawn comes, day dies, night falls. And yet no pointed pick comes to liberate him; there's no drill to prise the lock of his jail. He sleeps in the seams, ever quiet, ever nothing, ever vapour.

Treorchy news, 22nd December, 1990 – Maerdy pit closes.

At one time, there were over fifty pits in the Rhondda valley, making the area, synonymous with coal mining during the industrial revolution. Now, the last of those pits has closed. Maerdy's gates were locked for the last time. What future the local towns face is uncertain. Maerdy employed 2,024 men at its zenith in 1918, and even though that number has steadily dropped over the years, it is still thought that even this single closure will put considerable strain on the local economy.

Any day now. Time passes. More time passes. Dawn comes, day dies, night falls; dawn comes, day dies, night falls. Sleep.

PERIPHERY
Paul Lewis

I write this while I still have time. I can see them now, those fleeting grey preludes of death, glimpsed in the periphery of my vision as they dart past me in their hateful, taunting way.

Let me make it clear from the outset: this is my brother's story, not mine, though with his demise was sown the seeds of my own, our fates intertwined in death just as they were in life.

We were twins. Not identical in looks, though the resemblance was strong, and most definitely not identical in personality.

Jason was sensible, never doing anything without considering the consequences, whereas I tended to leap first, look later.

My brother lectured physics in Swansea University, not far from the house where we grew up. He was smart and could have gone far but chose to stay close to home even after our parents died.

I worked for a newspaper, an old-fashioned hack. I stuck around because I lacked the talent and drive to go further.

I am twice divorced. Jason never married.

We lived in the same city but rarely saw each other, staying in contact by emails, texts and the occasional phone call. We met up at Christmas, our birthdays and to mark the anniversaries of our parents' deaths. Yet no matter how distant we were in the physical sense, emotionally we remained close.

No, it was more than just close. As can be the case with twins we shared what I can only describe, for want of a less cliched expression, as a psychic bond. I could sense when there was something wrong. One minute, out of the blue, I would suddenly think of Jason. The next, the phone would ring and even before answering I knew it would be my brother calling.

I had one such intuition a fortnight ago. I was sure there was something amiss. I could have called him but that would have felt like an intrusion. Jason would call me if he had a problem he wanted to share.

A week or so later, that moment forgotten, I was on a day off and driving to Mumbles, a popular seaside village on the edge of Swansea. Jason lived close by and on impulse I decided to stop off to see him, telling myself it was not prying, just making the most of an unexpected opportunity. It was August. University was done for the summer so I knew there was every chance he'd be home. Sure enough his car was on the driveway.

I rang the bell and turned to enjoy the view across the broad expanse of Swansea Bay while I waited for an answer. The afternoon sky was cloudless. Sunlight scattered diamonds across the sea. Surely, I thought, there was no room in the world for anything bad on such a perfect day. Then Jason opened the door.

The look of surprise with which he greeted me could not disguise how pinched his face had become, or hide the dark circles under his eyes. He was pale, too, despite the heat wave that had tanned my face and arms a nutty brown.

My eyes were immediately drawn to the ragged scratch on his forehead, still raw and edged with blood. There were more scratches along both arms. I assumed he had been in an accident of some kind.

"Richard," he said, in a tone that made me feel more like a cold caller than his brother.

"This a bad time?" I asked, still taken aback by his appearance.

"No, no. I was just … Sorry. I was doing a bit of work.

Nodded off." He took a step back from the doorway. "Please, come in. Place is in a bit of a mess. Wasn't expecting visitors."

I followed him into the living room, where I looked around in dismay and some concern. Wrinkled clothes were heaped on both chairs, and dirty plates and dishes left on the floor. Jason had always been fastidiously clean.

"Have a seat," he said, indicating the sofa, which was clear of debris. He scurried around the room as he spoke, hastily gathering up the dirty crockery and carrying it out to the kitchen.

"Been so wrapped up with work I've let the place go," he called over the sound of running water. He hurried back into the room and grabbed handfuls of clothing. "Coffee?"

"Sure," I said, wondering if I should offer to help before deciding that would deepen his embarrassment. "Thanks."

"Back in a minute," he said, then disappeared out of the room again, taking the clothes upstairs.

As I waited I noticed there was something else out of place. A faint smell of cigarettes. Jason had smoked in his younger days but, as far as I knew, had given it up years ago.

He ran back downstairs. "Right," he said as he entered the room, clapping his hands together with such enthusiasm I knew I was witnessing a performance. From the kitchen I could hear a rumble as the kettle came to the boil. "I'll go and sort the drinks out," he said, and hurried off again as if he would explode if he slowed down.

I hadn't intended staying long. Now I could not leave until I had got to the bottom of his odd behaviour. He brought in two mugs of coffee and handed me one. I did not miss the way his hand trembled, or the way his eyes darted around the room. Whatever had happened, it must have been serious. Thoughts crowded round my head, demanding my attention. I ignored them. He was my brother. I could not bear to dwell on the dark explanations that suggested themselves.

"So how's tricks?" I asked casually as he sat in one of the armchairs. I wanted to give him the chance to confide in me before I had to ask outright.

"Oh, you know," he said vaguely, still nervously eyeing the room instead of looking at me. He rubbed one of the scratches on his arm. "Work piling up. Should have got on with it at the start of the holiday, not leave it all until the last minute."

I sensed that was a lie. But then he looked directly at me and gave me a fleeting smile that came close to breaking my heart.

"Maybe you need a break. There's still time for a holiday."

"I guess so. We'll see." He seemed to gather himself, obviously making an effort. "How are things with you?"

"The usual," I said, aware of his clumsy attempt to steer the conversation away from him. He was clearly volunteering nothing. I had to take the direct approach. "Mind if I ask a personal question?"

He was gazing around the room again. "Fire away."

"Has something bad happened?"

His hand jerked, almost spilling his coffee. He stared at me with an expression somewhere between shock and fear. Maybe it was because of the sunshine that streamed through the bay window but his eyes appeared to glisten, as though he was close to tears. "What?"

"Well look at you," I said. "It's not just the place that's in a mess, Jason. You are too. And what's with all those cuts? You been doing something you shouldn't?"

He shook his head. "I don't know what you mean."

"Come off it," I snapped back, concern giving way to mild anger. "I'm your brother. You can fool others but you can't fool me."

"Honestly. There's nothing wrong. It's just - "

"Don't give me any more crap about work. You've been doing the job long enough and you're bloody good at it." I realised I was almost shouting and lowered my voice. "Just tell me you haven't done anything stupid."

"Like what?"

Like drugs, I thought, or self-harming. I could not think of any other way he could have come by those scratches. But I said nothing, just fixed him with a level gaze until he looked away.

"You won't believe me," he said after a moment.

"Try me."

His eyes met mine, and I was taken aback by their fierce intensity. "I'm not just saying that, Richard. It's beyond belief."

"I'll be the judge of that," I answered. "Just tell me."

So he told me. And he was right. God help me, I did not believe him. I did not believe him until it was too late for both of us.

One warm night Jason lay awake in bed, listening to the soft scratching from the loft overhead. At first he managed to convince himself it was a bird, nesting in the eaves. Then, a few nights later, there came a rapid pattering back and forth along the floorboards, his nocturnal visitor having grown bolder and more inquisitive. That was when he had to accept it was a mouse, not a bird. The thought made him sick. He hated mice. Hated rats. Hated spiders too. The idea that a mouse could have got inside his home was as gross a personal intrusion as a tapeworm in his gut.

Mice were dirty. They carried fleas and diseases, or at least he assumed they did. Laying awake, listening to that darting, tapping movement, peering at the ceiling as if that would allow him to see through it, he itched in a dozen places and had to scratch them all.

He phoned the council the next day. To his dismay he was told the pest control team was run ragged because of the weather. A home visit would not be possible for another two days if he wanted to make an appointment. He did.

Afterwards he bought half a dozen mousetraps from the nearest DIY store. Not the snap-shut version beloved of cartoon animators but a green plastic wedge with a round hole at each end and a poisonous block at its centre.

Back home, heart thudding, he made himself check the attic.

He climbed the stepladder and pushed the hatch up, letting it fall back on its hinges in the hope the resultant crash would scare off any lurking rodent. The loft was silent. Slightly emboldened by this, Jason reached up and turned on the light, ready to dash back down the ladder at the first glimpse of movement. To his relief the attic appeared deserted, even if there was no shortage of boxes for a mouse to hide behind.

Jason pushed three traps against the nearest of them. Then he turned off the light, grabbed the edge of the hatch and pulled it into place before hurrying down to the landing.

He had to endure the sound of his unwelcome guest for two more nights before the pest control man turned up. By then Jason had inspected the external walls, trying in vain to determine how the mouse had got in. The exterminator, a cheerful type, red of face and with middle-aged plumpness, arrived in an unmarked white van. As Jason opened the door to him, he bellowed, "Got a moose in the hoose, have we?" in a mock Scottish accent, which made the anonymity of the van somewhat redundant.

The man did a cursory search around the house, then asked to check inside the garage. Within moments he had found where the mouse had got in. The garage was integral. In the side wall of the house, obscured by the garage door frame, was a crack between the bricks that had not been properly filled in.

"There's your problem," the exterminator said, poking a fingertip into the gap as if to prove the point. "If it's big enough to stick a pencil in, it's big enough for a mouse."

"I've put some traps down," Jason said, wanting to prove he was not entirely useless.

"Waste of time and money," the man said. "Might as well leave sweeties out for him. I've got some stuff in the van that will sort your little chum out, don't you worry about that."

What he had in the van was an industrial-sized tub of white pellets and four shallow plastic bowls. He filled and left two of the bowls in the garage and repeated the process in the attic. "Should do the trick but it might take a couple of days," he said. "Oh, and you might want to get some filler for that crack."

So Jason bought some sealant, which he used to plug the hole. It never occurred to him the mouse might still be in there. The sounds it made by night always stopped before dawn. He simply assumed the mouse went away, to wherever mice went to hide in the daylight.

He was wrong, as he discovered that night when he turned on the bedroom light and saw the tiny brown horror scurrying across the carpet towards the wardrobe.

Jason froze, fingers still on the switch.

The dirty little bastard must have come through the floorboards. For a moment Jason remained shocked into immobility. Then he was filled with a rage that surprised him with its sudden intensity and he lunged after it, wanting to stamp it into a squealing bloody pulp.

Anger turned to dismay when the mouse slipped under the wardrobe. Refusing to be beaten, Jason pushed the wardrobe so that it rocked on its rear edge, then let go. The weight of it falling back into place made the floor shudder. Before Jason had time to react the mouse shot out from beneath it, running over his foot before disappearing under the bed.

Chest heaving, soaked with sweat, Jason grabbed the bed and dragged it across the floor, revealing the lidded plastic boxes of books and DVDs he kept stowed beneath. He reached for the nearest of them and pulled. As he did, the mouse scuttled away from behind it, fur standing on end.

And then it vanished.

Jason had no idea whether it had run behind another box or found its way back under the floorboards. Neither did he have any intention of finding out. Leaving the light on and the bed where it was, he hastened out to the landing, slamming the door shut.

Next he went into the bathroom and grabbed some towels to block the gap beneath the bedroom door. He was determined to trap the mouse in one place. In his fury he was blind to the fact that it had other ways of getting around the house.

He spent the night on the sofa, feet dangling uncomfortably over the end. Between that and the unrelenting heat he became resigned to laying awake until dawn. At some point, however, he drifted off and remained dead to the world until sunlight on his face woke him. Opening his eyes, he realised he had forgotten to draw the living room curtains. He looked at the clock. It was almost nine.

He got up and went into the kitchen to boil the kettle, wincing at the smell of stale sweat. He should not have slept in his clothes but a vision of the mouse running over him had convinced him not to undress. There was nothing else for it. He would have to shower and get some clean clothes from his wardrobe.

Jason went upstairs and paused outside his room. The towels had not been disturbed so, unless the mouse had indeed gained access through the floorboards, it would still be in there. He briefly considered going down to the garage and getting the garden spade or some other impromptu weapon, then decided against it. The mouse offended him with its presence but it could not hurt him. By trying to hit it with something heavy he would probably end up damaging the room, its contents or both.

He pulled out the towels and opened the door.

Sunlight bathed the walls and the pale blue carpet, rendering the scene of minor carnage from last night's exertions almost surreal. Jason blinked. There, stretched out on the carpet, smaller, thinner and altogether more fragile than he remembered, was the mouse. It must have died of fright, he thought with a sudden grin of triumph.

Unable to bring himself to handle it, he went down to fetch the spade, shovelled up the tiny corpse and carried it at arm's length downstairs and out to the bin. Then he got out the Dyson and gave the room a thorough cleaning.

The sense of relief he felt was disproportionate. After all, the mouse had only been in the house for a matter of days. But Jason was a creature of habit. He liked his life to be orderly, to follow certain rules and procedures. He knew it was ridiculous, almost obsessive-compulsive, but equally he knew he would never change. It was the way his brain was wired.

Maybe he needed a holiday. It was something to think about. Certainly it was something his brother Richard often encouraged him to think about. Jason never usually felt the need. He liked walking and he liked the beach. When the weather was good he saw no need to leave Swansea. Yet the events of the last few days had rattled him in a way he suspected would take him time to recover from. A holiday? He would see.

That evening he sat watching TV, the sound turned low, the living room curtains partly drawn. The glass of wine in his hand was meant to help him relax but he ached with tension, his pessimistic side expecting to hear the scuttling and scratching resuming overhead at any time. Being sure the mouse was dead did nothing to unravel the knots his stomach was tied in.

As darkness fell Jason felt a tightening in his chest. His breathing began to sound ragged. It was around this time the mouse had made its presence known. Now on his third glass of wine, his head was buzzing but he remained rigidly attentive.

Then he saw movement along the floor in the periphery of his vision. At once he leapt to his feet, not even registering the wine that sloshed from the glass, spilling on the carpet. "Jesus," he gasped, while his heart threatened to burst from his ribcage.

Almost immediately, however, it became clear he was jumping at phantoms. Where he could have sworn he had seen movement was a corner without furniture. Had anything been there he would have seen it immediately. There was nothing.

Jason blew air from between his lips and sat back down. He rubbed the wine stain on the carpet with his foot and tried to focus on the TV but it was showing nothing that interested him. Most of the time he only put it on for company.

He saw movement again, the merest glimpse of motion out of the corner of his eye, this time from another part of the room. "Shit," he said, leaning forward and whipping his head around to try to catch sight of whatever it was before it disappeared. As before, he saw nothing. Sitting back on the sofa, he realised it was just his mind, playing games. Despite himself he was powerless to refuse to play along with it.

He went to the kitchen for more wine. As he opened the fridge door he imagined he saw a dark shape scuttle out of the shadows and into the living room. Whatever he thought he had seen was gone in the instant it took him to turn his head to follow it. Tension and wine combined to make him feel sick. Despite this, he would not stop drinking. It was the only way he could be assured of sleep.

This became a pattern that repeated itself over the next few nights, testing his resolve to the limit. Again and again he would be certain he had seen something moving rapidly across the room, always in the very extremes of his vision. Each ephemeral sighting gave rise to the same breathless sense of panic. He was trained in scientific discipline yet Jason could not bring himself to accept what the evidence pointed to; that they were mere illusions. He found he was drinking more, too, the alcohol a necessity rather than a source of pleasure.

After enduring another haunted night and having emptied two bottles of wine and started on a third, Jason fell asleep on the sofa.

The first thing he became aware of the next morning was the now-familiar pounding in his head, followed swiftly by the pressure on his bladder. It was only when he got up, groaning as the headache made a quantum leap in intensity, that he noticed the bloody gashes on his arms. He examined them once he had staggered out into the kitchen and taken the last of his painkillers, relieved he still had some left. He counted half a dozen scratches, each several inches long. Although not particularly deep, they hurt.

Frowning, Jason tried to see beyond the fog that filled his brain and figure out how he had got them. Surely they could not have been self-inflicted. He had never wanted to harm himself or anyone else. However, once he established the doors and windows were locked, he was left with no choice but to accept he had been responsible. Try as he did, though, he could not remember doing it. Nor could he find whatever blade he had used. Unless he regained his memory the cause would remain a mystery.

That disturbed him to the point where he felt unable to stay in the house, as if distrustful of his own company. Once showered and dressed he went out, making his way to the coastal path that led to Mumbles. Dense swirling mist obscured the bay, deadening sounds. For a few disconcerting moments Jason felt as though he was trapped in one of his own dreams. A shape barely glimpsed in the mist, that of a dark mass like an island a short distance offshore, reinforced that odd sense of displacement.

A cyclist overtook him at speed, snapping him out of his reverie. Before long the mist had gone, burned away by the midday sun, revealing nothing untoward offshore. Overhead was a brilliant blue vault devoid of clouds. Seagulls cackled and ranted as they sliced through the sky. By the time Jason reached Mumbles his hangover had gone. Sea air, he thought. A cure for everything.

Even the scratches no longer bothered him. They could have been inflicted in any number of ways. Maybe he had got them cutting back the overgrown garden yesterday, but had not realised it at the time. Or he could have scratched himself on something while staggering drunkenly around the house in the early hours.

He walked until he reached Mumbles Pier, then turned to make his way back. It was busier now, the promenade heaving with walkers and cyclists. He was glad to be heading home, preferring the village in the cold winter months when he almost had the place to himself.

Harsh light bleached the world and he wished he had remembered his sunglasses. By the time he neared home he was tired and thirsty. There was a faint throbbing behind his eyes that mushroomed into a resurgent hangover. Instead of going straight to the house he detoured to the Spar where he bought more painkillers and, despite the ache that had claimed the space between his temples, two bottles of wine. On impulse he also bought a pack of cigarettes. He was not a regular smoker but there were times when he craved the nicotine rush and this was one of them.

Home again, he put the wine in the fridge and took four painkillers, then sat in the living room with his eyes closed while he waited for them to kick in. Before they had chance to work he fell asleep in the chair. He remained asleep for two hours and would have slept longer were it not for the flaring pain that snapped him awake.

"Jesus, what?" he mumbled, his mouth and throat so dry the words were more croaked than spoken. He raised a hand to rub his eyes, which was when he saw the blood dripping from his wrist. Turning his arm revealed a long hairline gash that must have been deep to have bled so copiously. Frowning at it, Jason caught sight of a flitting motion from the corner of his eye. Then came a searing pain in his lower leg and he looked down to see a livid fresh scratch across his ankle. It too was bleeding heavily.

"What the *fuck*?" Jason lunged up from the chair, ignoring the agony from the wounds in his arm and leg. There was another fleeting glimpse, closer this time, and almost instantaneously something that felt like a razor sliced a gash across his forehead. He made a sound that was half gasp and half scream and bolted from the room, barging into the kitchen door in his haste to get out, half blinded by the blood trickling into his eyes.

The back door was locked and he fumbled with the keys for several panicky moments before he got it open. Then he ran the length of the garden, almost out of his mind with pain and confusion and fright. He was gasping for breath when he stumbled to a halt at the fence. This isn't possible, he told himself, repeating the thought again and again until it became a mantra in his head. Yet it provided no solace, for not only was it possible, it was happening and it was happening to him.

"Okay," he said, running a hand through his hair while he struggled to bring himself under control. "Okay."

Realising he could not stay there without attracting the attention of his neighbours, he returned to the house where he hesitated outside the back door. On the one hand he knew there had to be a rational explanation. On the other he was scared to go in. Something had attacked him. Not a mouse … it had moved too quickly to be a mouse and, though he had only glimpsed it, he had gained an impression of it being larger.

The open door beckoned. Still Jason hesitated. Then he saw the cigarette pack on the kitchen table and felt a sudden urge to smoke. He darted into the kitchen, remaining there just long enough to grab the cigarettes and the box of matches he kept by the gas oven.

Once outside he hurried away from the doorway and lit a cigarette with shaking hands. The taste of it was as vile as he remembered but he welcomed the rush like he would an old friend. He sat on a patio chair while he considered his next move, working through the options with characteristic thoroughness.

There was something in the house. Whatever he had seen was too big to be a mouse or even a rat. Having disregarded the supernatural, on the basis that there was a rational explanation for everything, he eventually concluded it was a neighbourhood cat that had got in through one of the upstairs windows he kept open in the warm weather. Maddened perhaps by the scent of the mouse it had turned on him, clawing him while he slept.

There were logic gaps in the theory one could drive a bus through. But in his desperation, and in the absence of a viable alternative, he seized on it like a drowning man grabbing hold of a lifeline.

So then. There was no reason to fear going inside. It was a matter of searching the house, making sure the cat had gone, and then closing the windows. His nights would be warm and airless but he considered that a small price to pay.

A strange sound like a roar in the distance made him look up sharply. It had sounded like it came from somewhere near the seafront. Intrigued, glad of the distraction, Jason dropped the cigarette and ground it out with his shoe, then set off to investigate.

The roaring came again, rumbling like an invisible freight train. Perhaps there had been an explosion in the steelworks across the bay, the sound carrying far without diminution on the still summer air. Jason hurried down the path to the side gate and through to the front garden.

What he saw almost stopped his heart with terror.

It was as if a photograph of our world had been overlaid with that of another, far stranger realm. Squatting in the bay like some grotesque toad was an island where no island existed. It was as black as coal and at its centre was a volcanic peak from whose glowing summit sulphurous clouds belched forth, obscuring the sun.

Winged creatures, like birds spawned by a nightmarish mind, circled the peak, while the island itself writhed as though alive from the multitude of grotesque beasts that crawled and lumbered across its surface.

Even from a distance Jason, held rigid by fright and by shock, could see these animals bore no resemblance to the fauna of our world. He saw a great many tentacles and a great many gaping maws. The sounds they made, keening and gibbering and howling, were a symphony of madness. And then came that dreadful roar again and a monster that dwarfed the others rounded the mountain. It walked on two legs like a man but its head was akin to that of an octopus. Scales clung to its rubbery body and long slender wings emerged from its back. It had claws on all four of its limbs.

The ground shook with each stride the thing took. It traversed the island in mere seconds before wading into the sea, sending a tsunami to engulf the shoreline. Even though he knew the creature had seen him and was heading his way, Jason could not move. He realised he was making a tremulous squealing sound, like a siren rising and falling. There was nothing he could do but watch in frozen, dumbstruck terror as the creature emerged from the bay, water falling from its scales like a series of cataracts. Its tentacles lashed back and forth. Then its hideous maw opened wide and another deafening roar emerged, making the world tremble.

Jason blacked out. When he came to, the creature and the island, along with its loathsome menagerie, were gone. The bay stretched out before him, looking exactly as it should. Jason, who had fainted onto the grass, head missing the bordering wall by inches, sat up slowly, not sure whether to laugh with relief or cry from sheer despair.

He had contrived an explanation for the scratches but could find no satisfactory explanation for his freakish vision. The island, the monster, that terrible roaring … none of it existed in the real world. He did not take drugs and was not an alcoholic, though he was drinking more than was good for him. So he was either losing his mind or experiencing something his scientific background allowed for but had in no way prepared him for.

He returned unsteadily to the back garden, where he sat chain smoking as he tried to come to terms with the unthinkable. He knew he was not going insane. Once he discounted the logical, all that remained was the illogical. The impossible truth.

There were any number of theories relating to parallel worlds; alternative dimensions, invisible realms that existed alongside ours. Jason was convinced he had somehow parted the veil between this world and another, a place where evolution had followed an entirely different path. As to the how of it, he could only imagine his revulsion and fear had been so intense as to create a heightened state of sensory awareness. So convinced was he that he had seen peripheral movement that did not exist in our world, he had somehow glimpsed movement that *did* exist in another.

If he could see them, it followed they could see him. Presumably he appeared as strange to these otherworldly creatures as they did to Jason. An intruder and therefore a threat. Their first reaction would be to attack.

So excited was he by the implications that he forgot to be afraid. He wanted to call his work colleagues, call his brother, call anyone who would listen. Yet no sooner had he thought this than it occurred to him he had no proof. Nobody would believe him. Had he heard the story from anyone else, he wouldn't have believed it either.

Jason looked down and was surprised to see a dozen or more crushed cigarette butts scattered on the patio around him. The light was fading, too, leaving much of the garden obscured by shadows. He looked apprehensively towards the house and wondered whether he could summon the courage to go inside. Just because he could not prove the truth of his story did not make it any less real. Whatever those creatures were, they were hostile and they were dangerous.

Then the world seemed to shift. He could find no other way of describing it. Away went the sky, obscured by sulphurous smoke, and the evening silence was shattered by a terrifying roar.

He needed no more persuading. Grabbing the cigarette pack and matches, he ran inside the house, to a night of sheer hell.

Jason's voice, which had grown increasingly hoarse as he related his story, now fell silent as if it had given up on him altogether. I stared at him. My brother appeared to have aged years in the time it had taken him to tell the tale. His head was lowered and his hair appeared sparser and greyer than I recalled. I wanted to go to him, to hold him, to tell him everything would be fine. Instead I did nothing but wait in silence for him to continue.

Finally he looked up and gazed at me with moist red eyes. "They were all over the house," he said, voice flat and dreadfully bleak. "There was no escaping them. Everywhere I went, those fucking things followed. They hurt me, Richard. I had no way of protecting myself. It was like trying to fight off smoke."

He wiped a hand across his mouth. "I couldn't leave either. I knew what was out there. That other place. That island. That *thing*. I was damned if I did, damned if I didn't. I swear to God, Richard, if I'd had a gun in the house I would have ended it there and then."

"No, you wouldn't," I said softly. Yet even as I spoke the words I found myself doubting them. I had never seen my brother like this. I had never seen anyone like this. I had no idea what he was capable of, just as I had no idea what to do.

"You do believe me, don't you?" He was almost pleading. "You know me better than anyone. You know I wouldn't make up something like this don't you?" He started to cry then, before quickly regaining control. "Because if I can't convince you, Richard, how could I hope to convince anyone else?"

"I believe you," I said.

He looked at me directly for a moment, as if searching for the lie behind the statement. Then, apparently satisfied, he nodded. "Well thank God for that. So what are we going to do?"

I did not have the first clue. My brother had suffered some kind of breakdown. Parallel dimensions, mysterious islands, giants with octopus heads ... it was all insane. The scratches were patently self-inflicted, even if his tightly curled fists meant I was unable to surreptitiously check his fingernails for blood.

"Well?" he demanded, his mood abruptly hostile.

I got to my feet, feeling a sudden urge to be away from there. I could not bear to be around this stranger masquerading as my brother a moment longer. Nervous breakdowns were not my specialty. I felt I needed professional advice.

Jason's eyes widened. "You're not leaving?"

"I have to," I said. "I need to think about this. Get help."

"But who can possibly help?"

"That's one of the things I need to think about." I had to steel myself against the stricken look on his face. While his story was utterly crazy I had no doubt he believed it. "I promise I'll be back as soon as I can. You'll be safe in the meantime."

"How can you say that? I told you, they're all over the house!"

"Then sit in the garden. Smoke a few cigarettes." I spoke to him as one might a difficult child. "You were safe there yesterday, yes?"

"Until I heard that roar and the island appeared."

"The island only appeared when you went looking for it," I said, turning his own twisted logic against him. "If you hear anything, stay where you are. If you can't see the creature, it can't see you."

He mulled this over for a moment. "Okay," he sighed, clearly unconvinced. "If you say so. But you promise you'll be back?"

"I promise. Just take it easy. Everything will be fine."

Those were to be the last words I would ever say to him.

The sun was low in the sky when I left. I had been in Jason's house much longer than I'd realised. It would be night soon. No wonder he was so frightened when he saw I was leaving. I drove home and sat in solitude with the lights off, sipping whisky, wondering what to do next. I tried not to think about my brother, who would be going through his own private hell right then. I knew I should have stayed with him, to expose his delusions for what they were or just to provide a shoulder to lean on. Yet, though I am ashamed to admit it, I had been repulsed by him, as if I feared his mental illness was a disease I would contract if I remained around him much longer.

More than anything, though, I felt helpless. I did not know who Jason's GP was and wondered if I should talk to my own, to see what he could suggest. But that would all take time and my brother needed urgent help, before he could cause himself serious harm.

Urgent help. The words pierced my brain like a knife. My brother needed urgent help and there I was, miles away, drinking.

I got up and poured the whisky down the sink, angry with myself. I should never have left Jason on his own. I had been selfish, so concerned about my feelings that I had lost sight of his suffering. I could picture him now, alone and afraid, sitting in the garden, cigarette in hand as if the smoke could somehow ward off evil.

Then I was struck by a terrible sense that something was wrong, a premonition magnitudes stronger than any I had felt before. My head whirled as I ran out into the hallway and grabbed my car keys from where I had left them on the stairs. Please God, I thought, don't let him do anything stupid. I wasn't conscious of driving, only of the horrific images that filled my mind, of Jason holding a knife to his wrist or his jugular, the blade slicing deep, conjuring blood...

I raced along the Mumbles road, not caring about speeding or being over the limit, Jason's safety much more important to me than my licence. I could only pray I was not too late. But then from a distance I saw the carousel of red and blue lights outside his home and I knew beyond doubt that my brother was dead.

My recollection of what happened afterwards is like a series of snapshots, each capturing individual moments that, when laid out in sequence, tell a story in essence if not in detail.

Police cars parked in the street. Blue and white tape sealing off the area around my brother's house. Neighbours, wearing curious and concerned expressions, talking in muted tones as they congregated outside the cordon. A policeman in uniform ordering me to stay the other side of the tape, grabbing hold of me when I ignored him. More cops running at me when I broke free and charged towards the house. A glimpse of a large ragged stain on the front window, dripping red in the flashing light. The grass rushing up to meet me when I was wrestled to the ground. And playing over these snapshots, like a soundtrack taped in hell, is the hoarse banshee wailing of my screams.

The newspaper reports merely hinted at the truth. The official police statement only confirmed that my brother had died from multiple wounds. Neighbours raised the alarm after hearing prolonged agonised shrieking from Jason's house several hours after I left. What the police did not, and never would, reveal was that he had literally been torn apart and that the doors and windows had all been locked from the inside.

Most of his body was gone. What little of it remained had been scattered around the living room, the walls, floor and window drenched in his blood. The police family liaison officer later admitted to me it was the most savagely violent case the investigating team had ever encountered, and the missing body parts had left them baffled.

But not me. I knew what had happened. In our world, we stand at the top of the food chain. However, in the twisted parallel dimension Jason had glimpsed, much bigger predators had evolved. His peripheral glimpses had been of that realm's equivalent of mice, only larger and more vicious.

And where there were mice there were cats…

He had shown himself, drawn attention to himself, made himself prey. That was why so much of his body was missing.

I kept my silence, knowing I would be dismissed as a lunatic in the same way as I had dismissed Jason. How I wished now, with the benefit of hindsight, that I had believed him at the time, not when it was too late, for me as well as for him.

Shortly after his death I began to catch glimpses of darting phantoms from the corner of my eye. This morning I woke from a troubled sleep, in which I dreamt I heard a distant roaring from the direction of the bay, to find blood on the sheets and scratches on my arms. I am terrified but I know not to repeat the mistakes that Jason made.

To draw as little attention to myself as possible I have remained indoors, largely confining myself to my study. There I have written this account so that others will know the truth of my brother's death. Whether they believe is another matter.

It will be dark soon. Time to save this file and shut down the computer. I will update my story tomorrow, if I survive the night.

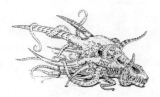

STRANGER CROSSINGS
RECLAIMING THE LOST LANDS
Adrian Chamberlin

It surely is no accident that the old Welsh name for England is "Logres", which translates as "The Lost Lands". And the creatures that came tonight...their name is so similar to that word for England. The lands were not lost to the English, but abandoned.

Perhaps there's truth in the rumour of the Welsh being survivors of a lost landmass in the Atlantic – all myths have a seed of truth in them. A spore, if you will, that lies dormant, waiting for the right moment – or even sheer chance – to allow it sustenance.

Some seeds take root; grow into wood and stone, just as the river crossing here did. This town has seen such sights – William the Conqueror crossed here on his way to be crowned King; Matilda skated under the very arches on the frozen Thames on her escape from Oxford and King Stephen; Stephen used the bridge to lay siege to Wallingford itself, and then five hundred years later another civil war, another king crossed it... battles and bloodshed, pursuits and crossings. But always *human*. Until now. Now, we came full circle: I witnessed strange pursuits and even stranger crossings.

Forgive any indulgences on my part. This is my last communication to humanity, so I want to leave something that proves I'm not a monster. I'm sure armchair psychologists reading the events of tonight in tomorrow's papers will gloat over my alcoholism and depression, my misanthropy, say that is proof that I was heading for a major psychotic episode. A bizarre combination of hayfever medication, antidepressants, and the ancient fungal spores tipped an already unbalanced mind into meltdown. I hope this will redress the balance.

We were about to succumb to the monsters the people who founded Wallingford thought they had vanquished. But who will believe me? They call me a murderer. The sirens of the emergency services have replaced the sounds of folk music and merriment of Wallingford's Bunkfest.

They're finally coming for me, but I have no intention of being taken into custody. For the spores of the Lloigor have taken root within me. My actions on the Kinecroft were not enough. I only banished the steeds, not the riders.

The petrol has soaked the books in my shop and filled the musty air with the smell of incipient holocaust, but still it won't banish the stench of the fungal spores. Every breath I take, every exhalation, is a reminder of what has been unleashed, and only fire will destroy it.

Was it only six hours ago that the August sunlight died and the shadow descended over my shop? The seeds of destruction transported from Wales by new horsepower.

I looked up through the opened door and sighed, recognising the unmarked white Luton van and its chubby driver. His window was down and I could just make out his face through the fog of tobacco smoke.

"Hey Taffy! What's occurring?"

Oh for God's sake. I took another swig of wine and groaned at the thought of rubbish he'd collected from his most recent house clearance assignment. Nick Glass had parked his Luton directly opposite my shop, only just missing the stack of bargain paperbacks I'd stacked. He swaggered in, his work shirt and combat trousers stained with sweat, stubbing his rollup on the porch as an afterthought.

I couldn't smell the usual stink of smoke on him, obtained from being cooped up for endless hours clanging off Marlboros in the cab. For once, I was thankful for my hayfever.

I saved my spreadsheet on the hard drive and pushed the keyboard drawer in. "Just because I was born in Cardiff doesn't make me Welsh. *You*, Mister Proud-To-Be-Born-In-England, are more Welsh than I am."

"Shut it, Taffy. I grew up in Wallingford. You don't get more English than that."

"Wallingford's a Welsh town," I replied with a grin. "You were born here, so that makes you Welsh." I never tired of this; when Nick wound me up about my Cardiff birth and launched into the "boyo", "isn't it", and "there's lovely" remarks I would take great pride in telling him about the South Oxfordshire market town's Welsh origins.

Is Wallingford Welsh? It was once known as "Wealhinga-ford" which some believe to be the name of an Anglo-Saxon leader – "ingas" means "people of", so Wallingford means "Wealh's people's ford". But other readings explain "Wealh" as the name of a group of early settlers from Wales, and that "Wealh's Ford" mean's "river crossing of the Welsh folk". And tonight's events have proven this to be the case.

"Started early, have you?" He pointed to my half-empty bottle of Merlot and peered over my shoulder. He shook his head, and I knew he'd seen the other bottle. Empty.

"So would you if you had to put up with all that shit out there." I jerked a finger at the window, now blocked by a dirty white van so he couldn't see the Morris Dancers cavorting in the Market Place. But we could hear them, and the sounds of their sticks banging together. "Arseholes. Wish they'd hit each other with those sticks."

"Wallingford's very own Bernard Black. No chance of any municipal pride or supporting the local community? Bunkfest could be another Glastonbury if it gets any bigger."

"Fine words from England's very own Nessa." I squirted two bursts of Beconase into my nostrils and sniffed, wincing at the chemical odour. I sneezed. "What do you want, anyway?"

"Need a favour." Nick scratched the stubble on his three chins. "The Luton's in for service and me missus won't let me store nothing in the gaff. Can I store the stuff in your back room? There'll be a score in it for ya."

I took my time refilling the wine glass. "Depends what you've got."

"Treasures from your country, Taffy. Llantrisant, to be exact."

I looked up. "Llantrisant?"

"Yeah. Bloke wanted his dead gran's cottage cleared quickly, wants to get it on the market."

"I see." Unexpected windfall from a relative he cared nothing for. Clear the house of all the personal effects in time for the estate agent to make a valuation. Quick sale of the property, not interested in whatever junk the old dear had stashed away in the attic. Nick sees this all the time in his line of work.

Some of the stories he told me used to break my heart. House clearances are nothing more than rubbish emptying with the occasional treasure hunt. But what is junk to one person is another's treasure – photos of passed away spouses, 1970s exercise books of children's schoolwork, from kids who've grown up and not bothered to visit the parents until the will is read out, china ornaments of cats and dogs, and cheap framed pictures of what looks like kitsch art but reflected someone's character, taste...personality.

And all thrown away, without even the courtesy of inspection from the heirs. Nick wondered why it always angered me so much. I couldn't help it; I remember all too well the petty squabbles of my Cardiff aunties and uncles fighting over the estate of my mum, not caring a bit for her when she was alive, not even bothering to visit her in the hospice when cancer riddled her. But as soon as she'd gone, they didn't so much crawl as erupt out of the woodwork.

Times were hard for Nick. The days of making a killing on eBay and the local antique shops are long gone; the inheritors aren't stupid, and neither are the executors. In the last few years Nick scraped pennies by selling the rarer deleted DVDs and vintage toys, but hadn't realised books are the real treasure. As much as Nick takes the piss out of me, we both know his business would've sunk if it wasn't for my eye for a rare tome or *object d'art*.

Nick wiped more sweat from his neck as the roller shutter

clattered up its runners. He squinted at the noonday sun as if it was full of maggots. "Plenty o' books for you to wank yerself silly over, Taffy. Hardbacks, gold lettering on the side."

I winced. "Please don't tell me they're *Readers' Digest*."

He grinned at that. "Nah, these look good, but I'll let you sort 'em out."

"After I get some fungicide," I sighed, eyeing the damp cardboard boxes with distaste. The sun beat down on the wagon, and the smells of badly-stored paper filled my nostrils. Mouldy. Musty. Unsellable. "Okay, what else?"

He took another drag, but didn't move. "Something that's rare as rocking-horse shit. Look for yerself."

The cartons weren't as badly damaged as I feared; they remained in one piece when I dragged them away from the bulkhead, but the fungoid smell was overpowering. Slick puddles of brown slime left trails on the Luton's floor. I held my breath.

Behind were a collection of broken dining chairs and an old camphorwood chest. The chest was adorned with Oriental figures, pagodas and bamboo trees, but heavily chipped and scraped. The metal hinge was missing. I slid the chest to one side, wincing at the cracking and splintering sound it made.

The blankets were old and threadbare, more used as packing material than bedding. I inspected the twine holding the rolls together and reached for my penknife. The bonds parted easily – too easily, stressed by the bulk they restrained – and the horse leapt at me.

It was like a hobby-horse – one of those old pieces of Victorian childhood, with a small wheel at the base and a carved horse's mane running up the pole. This was larger, the ash pole standing six feet high. The head was a standard, flat two-dimensional carving, with gaudy colouring and eyes created with that unsettling paintwork you see on dolls and nursery paintings of animals from this period.

What really surprised me was what Nick said next. "That's not the real head, mate. Check the camphorwood chest."

The sight of the horse's skull was initially alarming – Nick liked pulling rabbits out the hat, so to speak, and wanted to see me jump – but I don't think he'd expected the effect it truly had on me.

It was the skull that was the source of that musty, damp-stone aroma; the scent of ancient churches – or perhaps older sites of worship. The bone was ancient, without a doubt, but it had been…well, *maintained* is the only word I can think of. I rubbed my fingers after lifting the topmost section from the chest and saw traces of whitewash under my nails. The teeth – all intact, none missing – gleamed an unnatural white that could only have come from regular brushing. Even the eye sockets, starved of sight for untold centuries, lacked darkness.

And it was huge. The camphorwood chest was about two foot square – the skull only just fit within. I lifted the skull carefully, surprised by its lightness. I hadn't expected the mandible to be attached to the upper case – turns out it was wired by the back molars – and the jaws of the dead beast gaped in welcome. The teeth gleamed.

"A real monster, eh?"

An understatement. This thing could've dwarfed a shire horse.

The off-white sheets it had been packed in were coarse and smelled of museum displays. The bone certainly wasn't recent, but it made the accompanying paraphernalia of bells and ribbons seem positively recent. I inhaled, breathing in the aroma of ancient ritual and distant tradition. I imagined the wearer of this equine apparatus, garlanded with the small brass bells and green ribbons, dancing a jig as it advanced upon the stone cottages of the Welsh villages, seeking sanctuary before the Old Year died…

Nick checked his watch while I came back to the present. I shook my head, dispersing the after-images of the horse skull's eye sockets burned upon my retinas. They remained when I turned to Nick, superimposed upon his own eyes. I saw Death where he stood.

"Can't you smell it…Jesus. Whassup with ya?"

I blinked. "What d'you mean?"

"Your eyes, man. They look like you've been rubbing chilli powder in them."

I felt no discomfort, but my vision was blurred. "Pollen count's high today." Like I was going to tell him exactly what time this morning I had started drinking.

Or maybe it was spores from the mould. Spores...I closed my eyes and resisted the urge to rub my knuckles into them. The bliss of a false relief from the hayfever would last mere seconds before the barbed wire agony set in. I sneezed again and cursed myself for forgetting to pack the Opticrom eye drops. Just bear it, I told myself. At least summer wouldn't be for much longer.

"I'm surprised that Llantrisant bloke didn't keep it," I said as we carried the camphorwood chest through to the back room. "It's a heritage piece, the Mari Lwyd."

"The what?"

The Mari Lwyd – the Grey Mare. A Welsh Christmas tradition, one I thought had died out completely. I explained to Nick the role of this hobby-horse – how it headed up a party of Yuletide revellers who sing riddling songs to obtain entrance to houses, and if the occupants are unable to cap the rhymes the Mari Lwyd enters and must be fed. Nothing sinister, just a weird version of Christmas carolling. It was peculiar to the valleys of South Wales, but I grew up in the slums of inner-city Cardiff, and my childhood home had never been visited by the Grey Mare.

"Why a horse?" Despite his slouched pose, there was a gleam of interest in his eyes.

Why indeed? The Christian tradition has it that the grey mare was kicked out of the stable in which Christ was born and searches until the end of time for a place to stay. The Celtic connection was probably to the cult of the horse goddesses Rhiannon or Epona.

"The horse was seen as a symbol of power and fertility," I explained, "and animals that had the power to cross between this world and the otherworld were traditionally grey in colour. Or white."

And the veil between this world and the dark country was at its thinnest in the darkest time of the year, allowing entities from the otherworld the opportunity to cross over. Perhaps the Mari Lwyd was a symbolic way of paying respect to the "undiscovered country" as well as proving humanity's strength and intelligence in beating back the denizens of the dark.

The chest and the mast waited for me in the stockroom while Nick drove to the garage for his MOT. The boxes of books he'd "donated" to me – yes, all Jeremy Clarkson "bibles" and *Readers' Digest* hardbacks – were covered in black bin bags, ready for transporting to the tip. My assessment of their worth was correct – and these *hadn't* been affected by mould. The true treasure now lay before me.

My research confirmed what I already knew: this skull was abnormally large for any breed of horse. Using an online equine conformation tool I worked out the ratio of the horse skull to the body. It meant the beast would have been a whopping thirty hands high – at least twelve higher than the largest draft horse today. Three metres tall.

There was something else: on some horses there sits a canine on the maxilla, on the bar between the incisors and the squared molars. This canine – or "wolf tooth" as some referred to it – is rare in domestic horses. A relic of the first premolar, perhaps...but there is no more than one on each bar.

This had three.

There were no other abnormalities to the skull itself, aside from an incision in the maxillary bone to allow the tip of the mast entrance. I peered closely, seeing old material doubtless used as wadding to prevent the masthead breaking through the skull. Older even than the sheets that act as the shroud for the Mari Lwyd; this material was crumbling, powdering like chalk.

Intrigued, I unwrapped the mast from its bundle of rags and marvelled at the smoothness and lightness of the six-foot pole of ash; a perfect complement to the unnatural horse skull. The carved, flat masthead easily slid into the incision at the rear with a click like teeth clamping together, and I realised the horsehead shape wasn't an affectation – it was designed to hold the skull firmly into place.

There was a wire loop on the mast that hooked into the lower jaw, and a cord pulley system enabled the bearer to raise and lower the mandible at will. I couldn't resist; I raised the mast, the horse skull brushing the crumbling plaster of the ceiling, and activated the pulley three times.

The clatter of perfectly maintained molars clamping together was amplified by the tapering nasal bones, so it came out as a strange fluting sound. Only the incisors and the canine on the bar made the distinct *snap-snap-snap!* sound, which echoed around the bookcases. A chill descended, along with the dust from the wadding within the skull. Those incisors surely were not designed for cropping grass. Those, and the "wolf's teeth", were there for another reason.

I lowered the Mari Lwyd and propped it in the corner of the stockroom. I brushed the plaster and dust from my shoulders and scalp, wrinkling my nose at the smell of ancient bone and mould. I stared up into the eye sockets, no longer gleaming.

I sat back in my chair with a fresh glass of wine, rubbing the bridge of my nose in a subconscious effort to stop the ever-present irritation in my sinuses. The itching was different, harsher, as though I had snorted powdered glass. I sniffed, snorted, and then blew my nose. I stood and went to the stockroom to lock up.

Usually I ball the tissue and throw it into the waste bin. This time I glanced at the contents, the tissue trembling in my hands. There were streaks of blood in the mucus.

I stared at the dust on my shoulders, the overly white powder so similar to that which spilled from the nasal cavities of the Mari Lwyd. Similar in scent as well; I sniffed my fingers and then inhaled the fungous odour emanating from the ancient skull. I dropped the balled tissue.

Spores. Oh, Jesus...

"What the hell are you?"

In reply, the mandible dropped and the beast's maw gaped at me. Then the Mari Lwyd advanced. I started, momentarily panicked, until I realised the jaw had merely loosened itself from the pulley mechanism, and the shift in weight had upset the balance of gravity.

I put out a hand to halt the thing's fall. Perhaps I was more tired than I realised, but when the pole met my outstretched hand it felt heavier; the Mari Lwyd slammed into my palm. I grunted in surprise, and my own centre of gravity was upset. I was forced back, and my ankle collided with the binbag-wrapped books from Wales. It was that made me stumble and fall, had me crashing to the floor and cracking my own skull on the door jamb, just as the ancient skull came rushing to meet mine, the white, chalk-like powder disgorging from its mocking jaws...

I have only been knocked unconscious once before in my life, the result of a drunken argument with some thuggish lout from the Town Arms who objected to me quietly reading a book in a pub full of Manchester United kit-wearing chavs glued to the football on the big screen. An argument I lost, needless to say. But what I remember most of that night is the surreal and terrifying dreams that followed.

Not so much the content of the nightmares, more the feeling and heightened sense of reality that accompanied them. It was that same sensation of translocation and hyper-reality that I bore with me to the land of sleep. And the mares truly were of the night.

I stood alone upon a snowbound riverbank. The river was nothing but a morass of slush and churned snow, fighting against the current. The cut of the banks and the width of the river looked familiar, but it was the absence of the eighteenth-century arches of the bridge I cycled over every morning to work from Crowmarsh that baffled me, initially prevented me realising I was on the riverbank of Wallingford. Gone was the courtyard of The Boathouse opposite, gone too the slender spire of St Peter's Church. I turned, and as far as my eyes could see the landscape was barren, featureless, coated in pristine snow.

I shivered, a double chill cutting through me, because the snow and ice were real - my feet were frozen in my trainers and the and my skull throbbed with the leeching effect of the wind – and Wallingford had a bridge, had indeed been a river crossing, since Roman times, if not before.

There was no crossing. There were no signs of habitation. I looked into the steel-grey sky and saw nothing but the promise – or threat – of more snow to come. I shuddered, my teeth chattering violently. I hugged my chest, straining to keep whatever body warmth I could from being leeched from the T-shirt and jeans I was wearing when still in the bookshop.

The wind howled in my ears, became alternately a mournful howl and a shriek of triumph, of unnatural glee at the prospect of feeding on a sole human being.

I sank to my knees and buried my head in my hands, crying. I smelled that awful stench of fungus on my fingers, the mould that had issued from the mouth of the Mari Lwyd. The howl became louder, deafening, and I could discern a strange rhythm to it; an alternating pattern, that would have been a chant if uttered by human vocal cords. Something utterly inhuman…and yet, disturbingly familiar. Somewhere, I had heard this before.

I looked up and saw the very snow itself whirl into waves that swirled around me, rising and falling in time with the inhuman song. They coalesced, condensed, took humanoid form. I couldn't make out true shape of the three beings that towered above me, but a fiery glow emanated from each, giving form and texture to their faces.

Three scarlet circles upon each sloping snout. Three burning eyes illuminated the broad, tapering nasals and gave unholy illumination to the incisors and wolf's teeth in the maxillary bones. The jaws gaped, issued fire and spat fresh, blinding white powder at me. Not snow, but a powdery, chalk-like substance that reeked of fungus and ancient stone, and I realised with horror I was surrounded by three of the creatures, each of which owned a skull like the unnatural cranium upon the Mari Lwyd in my shop.

I leapt to my feet, the cold forgotten, running blindly. Ice chips pelted my eyeballs and tears streamed from my sockets, salt tears and unendurable cold blinding me. I pushed past one of the horses, and felt solid muscle and horseflesh, warm fur and hot blood. It uttered a cry like a horse's whinny, but amplified and echoing like the howls that could only have issued from prehistoric beasts on the arctic tundra. A huge foreleg lifted from the snow, three feet of damp fetlock appearing, coloured grey-brown with churned mud and clay soil, and I realised with fresh horror the beasts were even taller than I had assumed – the sheer weight of them had pressed their limbs into the ground.

No, not just their weight, but that of their riders. As the mount reared above me, its hoofs glittering with a steel-like mineral that turned them into edged ploughshares, I caught a brief glance of the entity mounted on the grey nightmare.

A glimpse, merely a second, but a brief moment in time that stretched to eternal, endless eons, as my human mind struggled to comprehend the alien being atop the nightmarish mount.

The ground sloped beneath me and suddenly gave way. I was up to my midriff in churning, semi-liquid winter; the frozen river claimed me. I went under and steel bands of cold crushed my ribcage, squeezing out the last of my air. The grey slush above me began to freeze instantly, the alternating patterns of light and dark ice refracting the alien light from the mounts' eyes – three-lobed, burning eyes – and the rainbow-hued auras of their riders, turning my icy tomb into a kaleidoscopic hell.

It was ice that carried me to a second unconsciousness, but it was fire that brought me back. The heat from an August sun burned my eyes as painfully as three-lobed orbs of those monstrous horse-creatures.

Crystal blue sky replaced the tarnished, grey, lowering storm clouds of my dream – or vision. Diesel exhaust fumes replaced the twisting, writhing snow patterns. And Nick Glass stood before me, now blocking the setting sun, as tall and imposing as the beasts on the frozen riverbank.

"You really should stay off the booze, mate." He held a Clipper to his rollup, disapproval on his face. "You wanna kip in your stockroom, that's your business – but try not to shag the merchandise, yeah?"

I rubbed my forehead, wincing with the sudden pain that throbbed in my temples. My mouth was stale and furry, and my nostrils were blocked. I felt like I'd been on an all-nighter, but…I lowered my hand and squinted at Nick.

"What d'you mean?" I winced again, this time at the pain in my throat and the hoarse voice that emanated from it. "I love books, but not in *that* way."

Nick thrust a thumb over his shoulder at the source of the diesel fumes. I tilted my head and saw an ancient, rusted Dormobile. Hammerite paint finish and mud were probably the only things keeping it together. Or perhaps the spray-painted stars and moons were blessed by Merlin or Gandalf, or something. Threadbare curtains twitched in time with the misfiring engine, and a thick bearded face smiled through the tobacco-smeared driver's window. A leisurely thumbs-up from the owner and a quizzical look at me and then the vehicle roared and spluttered, bumping off the kerb and driving away, its rattling exhaust pipe spewing more fumes that swirled over the kerb and into my stockroom. I coughed and turned my head, and then I realised the Mari Lwyd was gone.

"I almost lost the sale, thanks to you." He had to shout over the roar of the misfiring engine. "They came in the same time I did, and saw you sparko on yer back, the hobby-horse on top of ya."

"Wait a minute...go back. I'm missing something. You telling me you found a buyer already?" I rubbed the back of my head. An egg-sized bruise had decided to make its presence known to me.

"Yeah. I put the photo and a shout-out on the Bunkfest Facebook page. Got a reply straight away." He beamed, patting his shirt pocket and the wad of twenty pound notes it contained. "Five hundred notes they paid."

I took a deep breath and decided to chance getting to my feet. "Thanks for the concern for my health, Nick. I'll remember you in my will." The floor swayed beneath me and the doorway tilted, but I managed to stay upright. "Who's 'they', anyway?"

Nick shrugged. "A three-piece on the bill tonight. 'Stranger Crossings' they call themselves."

I stood in the doorway. Red, failing sunlight bathed my face and the stink of hippy van exhaust fumes faded. The air smelled sweet and summery again, but the prehistoric winter stayed in my mind and the chill remained in my body. My teeth chattered.

"Shit, man, you do look ill. Want me to run you over to

the doc's?"

"No, I'll be okay." That remained to be seen, but the mystery of Nick's buyer now took precedence, and temporarily banished the cold from my mind. I turned to him, standing in the space I had parked the Mari Lwyd. Despite Nick's bulk, that section of the stockroom looked empty, bare, now the six foot ash pole and alien horse skull had gone.

"They needed it tonight?"

Nick looked up and shrugged, folded his arms defensively. "Nothing sinister about it. They told me they've been looking for another Mary's Fluid to match their other two."

Other two?

I went into panic mode. The mention of two other Mari Lwyd structures that matched the third Nick had sold filled me with dread. No longer the annoyance that a calculating gyppo hiding behind the folky façade of a dance group knew the value of rarities more than I did, but the memory of what I had dreamed - no, not dreamed, *experienced*.

Three mares. Three riders. It couldn't be a coincidence. That hallucination – that *vision* – was telling me something.

"What else do you know about this lot?"

Nick frowned. "A fusion of Welsh folk dance and Tibetan monk chanting, or something. Having a launch of their first album next week, and the Bunkfest is their first live act. Chrissakes, man, what are you so wound up about? Google 'em if you're so bothered."

Stranger Crossings' website told me nothing. Just tour dates, which only included microfestivals like the Bunkfest – it'd be a while before they got to headline V Festival, Reading or Glastonbury, and with their repertoire it was hardly surprising. Welsh folk and Tibetan chant fusion, for God's sake. No wonder they were sharing the Saturday Night slot with sea-shanty act Short Drag Roger.

I sneezed on the keyboard, alarmed at the fresh blood that mingled with mucus on the keyboard. There was more than last night, and the smell of ancient stone and overpowering fungi returned. That only fired me further. I continued tapping and clicking away, ignoring the slimy stickiness of the keys and mouse buttons.

Basic photos and bios of the members – again, nothing special. Three hippy types in their early forties, all with middle-class first names and surnames that had to have been made up: Tarquin Leng, Quentin Lemuria, and Julian Kardath. Travellers in both sense of the word: - what most of Wallingford would call hippies – and globe-trotters with the visa stamps of far-off countries that only the well-off could afford, or would want to visit.

Links to iTunes and Amazon to preorder their album. The track listing of *Lloigor of Logres* was a bizarre list of Welsh and Oriental names. "The Lament of Y'Ha Nthlei"; "The Cloak of Tawil at-Umr"; "The Sighs of Anwynn"; "Shadrach's Hybrids"; "Tcho-Tcho Llamas Day"; "Y Fari Lwyd"…

There! "Y Fari Lwyd" – the Mari Lwyd Song. There was an option to play a sample. I clicked the window and a trio of badly harmonised male voices filtered through the speakers.

*"If there are people here
Who can summon Lloigor,
Then let us hear them now
Then let us hear them now
Then let us hear them now
Tonight."*

Nick snorted. "Well, at least they translated it. Can't see that stuff flying off the shelves, somehow – hey! Where y'going?"

I couldn't answer. I couldn't stop. I had to get to Stranger Crossings before they started their set. What I would say to them, how I would try to convince them not to play anything I hadn't considered.

My head pounded, as hard as my feet on the pavement. The evening heat beat down on me, oppressive and doom-laden. My eyes itched and I no longer needed to heed the warning of avoiding the hayfever-rub – the thought of further grinding the spores into my eyes turned my stomach to ice water.

The song played in my ears. The words weren't part of a

harmless folk-ritual; the tune they were sung to was *the exact same music* the alien riders of those monstrous steeds sang in my visitation,

In the Market Square strangers and townsfolk alike stared at me as I pushed past them. My eyes streamed with tears and side curtains of crimson appeared in my peripheral vision, threatening to close. Stilt-walkers waded through the mass of humanity like the night mares of my visitation, obscuring the Town Hall. The War Memorial loomed above me, the brass statue holding out the wreath like a noose. The flint walls of St Mary's Church caught the sunset and writhed like huge grey maggots, the mortar flashing horizontal streaks of scarlet; cemented with blood.

I cried in despair, and thin serpents of blood writhed from my nostrils, falling to the cobbles in thick spots like heavy rain. I coughed, spat, and felt steel bands tighten around my ribs. The curtains drew closer and the song filled my mind.

People gave me a wide birth as I half-ran, half-stumbled towards the Kinecroft. The green field was a riot of colour and motion; flags of all nations fluttered in a light breeze from the performance and beer tents; vintage steam engines, their black iron shining like ebony, puttered around the green; yeasty smells of micro-brewery ales mingled with the scents of burgers and noodles, but they couldn't overcome the stench of blood and putrid fungus in my nostrils.

> *"Well, gentle friends*
> *Here we come*
> *To ask may we have leave*
> *To ask may we have leave*
> *To ask may we have leave*
> *To sing."*

The chant was no longer in my head. I heard it: three male voices, singing in close harmony. I followed the direction of the singing, to the Kinecroft Big Stage, and my heart sank.

Like tall ships sailing into harbour, three horse skulls floated above the stilled mass of humanity in their sails of white shrouds, supported by spars of ancient wood.

"If we may not have leave,
Then listen to the song
That tells of our leaving
That tells of our leaving
That tells of our leaving
Tonight."

The sky greyed; the sun became a tarnished silver disk that skulked behind thunderclouds. My head spun. I sank to my knees and my coughing turned to retching; vomiting. A thick growth squatted before me, grey and fungous; the myriad bright rubies of blood were eyes of scarlet that swivelled and faced me. It shuffled, oozing over the grass like a monstrous slug. I cried out and backed away, colliding with a young mother pushing a double-buggy. She sneered at me with browned teeth and orange skin, the Union Flag tattoo on her flabby forearm writhing, taking the form of a starfish with a three-lobed, burning eye. The pallid creatures in the twin-buggy stirred, throwing off their coverlets with limbs that divided and elongated, became a thrashing mass of tendrils.

I kicked the double-buggy over and heard mewling, more an alien cry of unsatisfied hunger than an infant's pain and fear. The festival-goers' faces were masks of inhumanity and hatred; spongy, bloated and pallid. Red pinpricks burst open upon the cheeks of one market trader, the same scarlet eyes that watched me from the vomited, bleeding fungal spawn behind me.

Cries for my arrest mingled with the hiss of steam and *thud-thud-thud* of traction engines. It wasn't too late; I knew this was merely a trick of the poison spat from the desiccated brain of the Mari Lwyd; hallucinations, visions, to stop me reaching the dance act who would unwittingly recall those extra-terrestrial riders of the night mares.

Before me was a stall selling carved Green Man icons and didgeridoos added to the sense of alien invasion. Gargoyles and golems, serpents and demons, all hissed at me from their cold prison of stone, but felt more welcoming than the hostile humanity massing behind me. White powder fell from the skies and drifted over their distorted faces. It may have been snow; it may have been spores.

A wooden staff, carved from weathered oak into the semblance of a curved spinal column and surmounted with a horned demonic head, fell into my hands. I hefted it, swung it in an arc, smiling with satisfaction at the weight and the prospect of damage it would do to skulls. A monster to destroy monsters.

> *"If you've gone to bed too early*
> *In a vengeful spirit,*
> *Oh, get up again good–naturedly*
> *Oh, get up again good–naturedly*
> *Oh, get up again good–naturedly*
> *Tonight."*

There was a sudden hush from the audience as I approached the Big Stage. The crowd parted to allow me to clamber up onto the apron.

The three horse skulls turned on their poles to face me, their shrouds billowing. The stage lights flashed and rotated, turning the three Mari Lwyds into a riot of scarlet and blue. My eyes streamed again, and the sapphire lights coalesced, formed above the unholy mares.

The Lloigor. The riders from beyond the stars.

I felt that same icy chill as last night. The sky was steel-grey, threaded with glittering lines of silver. The seasons in reverse; this unholy summoning was to take place in a summer festival via a midwinter tradition.

A town created by Welsh settlers, now to be re-invaded by monstrous beings from beyond prehistory, from beyond the stars, hiding behind the figures of Welsh folklore.

And me, the only Welshman in Wallingford, given knowledge, *awareness* of these creatures, by some strange act of chemistry between the spores of the horse-beast's desiccated brain and my hayfever medication. The Lloigor could only walk the earth with hybrid beasts, which span the gulf of life and death; have the physical characteristics of the beasts of elder worlds.

I swung the demonic staff with a grin, aware of the blood

pooling in the bared lips. It tasted good.

It felt good. The staff swept in a horizontal arc, cutting the lead Mari Lwyd down in a flurry of shrouds and shattering spars. I inverted my staff and brought the demon head crashing onto the downed Mari Lwyd. The skull cracked easily enough, the mandible cracking and the maxillary bone spitting out its wolf's teeth and alien incisors, and the powder disgorging from the snout to reveal the cavity of a third eye. I fancied I saw a flare of scarlet in each of the orbs, flashing to create a single three-lobed, burning eye.

But there was something solid within. I frowned, wondering why this skull didn't disgorge the spores of its ancient, withered brains. I brought the staff crashing down again, and again. The cry of horror from the crowd reminded me of my position: headlining the Wallingford Bunkfest!

My vision faltered once more, the scarlet curtains threatening to close over my stage completely. That was why I saw blood in the crevasses of the horse skull.

The second Mari Lwyd, then the third. Each told the same story. There was something muffled from the second one, something that almost sounded like a human whimper of pain. I shook my head and brought the staff upon it.

I looked up. The revolving stage lights had ceased, and the power supply was cut off. There was silence throughout the Kinecroft, and a parting in the storm clouds allowed a golden ray of sunshine – *summer* sunshine – to bathe me in a natural spotlight of glory. The sapphire mist and incandescent, kaleidoscopic clouds had gone.

I took a bow, and crossed the stage.

It may seem incredible to you that no one tried to stop me, when they were calling for my blood not ten minutes previously. I was no longer myself, buoyed with the sense of triumph and self-satisfaction. Of course I kept the demon staff with me, and perhaps that made them hesitate.

No. Even on the walk back to my shop, I passed stunned festival-goers. Security staff in hi-vis jackets froze, made no attempt to stop me, despite what they had witnessed. Walkie-talkie sets blared and hissed static, and police officers at the gate by the Coach and Horses shrank from my approach.

With each step my euphoria faded, for the streets of my hometown took on a strange hue. The scarlet curtains had drawn closed, yet I could see – even more clearly. My vision was more defined, hyper-real, as though the inner fire burning within had given me unique powers of sight. It was only the beginning. Soon, I would see beyond the mere three dimensions we're limited to.

There was no pain in my chest or head, no short breath or wheezing from my lifelong hayfever. My limbs felt stronger, and I walked taller. It was only when I realised my limbs were taking me to the river that I realised my body was not moving off its own volition. There was a sense of anticipation, of a hunger that I couldn't quantify, that was taking me to the ancient site that the creatures had tried to cross millennia before.

When I changed my destination I felt resistance, my body twisting and writhing uncontrollably, as though alien puppet masters pulled on the strings and forced me to dance to their tune.

Every step back to the bookshop was agony. I clutched the staff like an arthritic old man, jabbing the base into the ground with each step as though steering a path through arctic ice, fearful my step would fail at any moment. The howls of prehistoric ice storms filled my ears and took the rhythm of my visitation before.

My vision misted, became human again, and seeped in blood. I staggered into St Mary's Lane, my staff now a blind man's walking stick, tapping, tapping, feeling my way home.

It has been an hour since the events on the Kinecroft. I feel the urge to leave, to head for the river. The Lloigor tried a new tactic; they whispered soft promises of conquest, of my fellow man under my yoke forever. I'm not fooled – I know I'll only be a slave myself. Why deny what little humanity I have?

Now they promise me a new form, to leave my humanity behind, to become one such as them. It is that offer that has kept me to the keyboard, writing out this email, committed to my final task.

I'm glad I kept the old CRT monitor. It shows constantly what I saw in my shop door window, reminds me of what I am becoming. The fire within reflects clearly, flames lapping at the third eye in the centre of my forehead.

Made in the USA
Charleston, SC
24 February 2014